GLADIATOR ISLAND

The Main Event

COREY O'NEILL

E

EPIC
Press

The Main Event
Gladiator Island: Book #2

Written by Corey O'Neill

Copyright © 2017 by Abdo Consulting Group, Inc.

Published by EPIC Press™
PO Box 398166
Minneapolis, MN 55439

Cover design by Laura Mitchell
Images for cover art obtained from iStockPhoto.com
Edited by Leah Jenness

LIBRARY OF CONGRESS CATALOGING-IN-PUBLICATION DATA

Names: O'Neill, Corey, author.
Title: The main event / by Corey O'Neill.
Description: Minneapolis, MN : EPIC Press, [2017] | Series: Gladiator Island ; book #2
Summary: Still reeling from his first fight in the island's gladiator arena, Reed must figure out
   who he can trust in this nightmarish place. If Reed isn't able to determine a way off the
   island soon, he knows he'll eventually be pitted against Odin, a physical specimen and expert
   fighter, who's wanted Reed dead since the moment they met.
Identifiers: LCCN 2015959398 | ISBN 9781680762686 (lib. bdg.) |
   ISBN 9781680762891 (ebook)
Subjects: LCSH: Adventure and adventurers—Fiction. | Interpersonal relationships—Fiction. |
   Survival—Fiction. | Human behavior—Fiction. | Young adult fiction.
Classification: DDC [Fic]—dc23
LC record available at http://lccn.loc.gov/2015959398

EPICPRESS.COM

For Leo,
always quick with a hug

CHAPTER 1

Inside this new cell, I was helpless as I watched the events in the Coliseum unfold in high definition on the television that sat on the table before me. The camera switched from a long close-up of Delphine to a tighter shot of Rose, who was in tears. Gareth's voice cut through the noise of the crowd's taunts and Rose's crying.

On the TV, I got a look at Gareth in extreme close-up. He was handsome, with thick salt-and-pepper hair, olive skin, and dark eyes. Now I totally saw the resemblance to his daughter Chelsea and how they both conveyed the same air of likable cockiness. The men and women in the crowd all shushed each other as Gareth continued speaking.

"Would you just look at Delphine? She is a sight for sore eyes, isn't she?" He addressed the spectators in the seats that flanked where he and Chelsea sat, and everyone clapped. "The girl may be a petite little thing, but her size belies great strength and ferocity, you'll see."

He turned to his left to look at Chelsea, who was smiling widely, and put his arm around her, laughing. Delphine's face was flushed red with anger; I recognized that look from our experience of being bullied by Titus on the boat.

"Rose, Rose, Rose—why are you trembling?" he called down to my former Ship Out mate as she cried loudly, turning her head every direction to scan her surroundings. "What a delicate and sweet one, just like her name."

She looked like a child, barely holding onto her sword in the middle of the Coliseum floor, as if its weight was too much to handle. Her arm quivered, her eyes were bloodshot, and tears streaked down her painted cheeks.

"What do you think, friends? Isn't it time we put her to the test and see if this delicate flower has any thorns?" Gareth asked.

Rose gazed at the spectators who were now chanting her name. I heard laughter coming from many different men; everyone looked relaxed and many were smiling. I estimated there were about forty spectators from Praeclarus, each draped with a golden sash over their chest, along with more than a hundred other people whom I guessed were probably prostitutes, trainers, White Suits, and other island staff. People were eating. Some men gnawed on turkey legs or sandwiches and took gulps out of frosty mugs of beer.

The thing that tripped me out the most was that they all looked so relaxed—as if this was just another day at a baseball game or something.

Delphine stood with her shoulders upright, a halo of sunlight at her back, but I saw she was now biting at the corner of her lip. Even in this moment she looked pretty, her green eyes set and determined, like she was trying to conjure an expression that said she didn't give a fuck. It surely wasn't true, but she was good at faking it.

Since I knew the truth of what was about to happen, I wished more than anything to escape the room to find a way to grab both Delphine and Rose and take them far away from here. I limped to the door and tugged it as hard as I could with my good arm. It was a pointless exercise, but I was desperate to do something, anything to try to help. I attempted to pace in front of the TV, but my shoulder and leg ached in pain, so I collapsed back onto the couch, defeated.

Delphine and Rose were positioned much the way Carl and I were at the start of our fight, about twenty yards away from each other and directly below where Gareth and Chelsea sat on their thrones.

I knew something—or someone—was directly

off-screen to force the girls to fight each other, just like the fire-shooting White Suits that triggered Carl to finally charge me. Just like us, they wouldn't attack each other unless they were provoked to fight for their own lives.

Gareth needed to put the fear of death in people in order to get ordinary teenagers to attack, and then kill, their opponents and their friends. I understood the only reason Carl attacked me was the fear he felt while trapped on the Coliseum floor, struggling for his own survival. And the only reason I retaliated and stabbed him was because he attacked me. Provoked, we became like wild animals, gouging and scratching in a panicked fight to live another day. And now, here I was—alive, but a prisoner. Both fates were unbelievable.

The scene with Carl repeated again and again in my head on a loop, like a video game level I played too many times. I pictured Carl on fire, then dropping to the ground to snuff himself out before charging at me with his spear outstretched.

I saw him running forward with that look of panic on his face, his eyes bright with recognition of the possibility of imminent death.

Now as I watched Delphine and Rose on the TV, my stomach hurt. Rose, full-on sobbing with snot dripping out of her nose and into her mouth, looked up at Gareth and yelled out, "Help me! Please! I'll do anything! Anything!"

This plea made the people in the crowd cheer even more, and she continued to scream, louder and more desperate, until her cries devolved into blubbering, incoherent shrieks. Gareth looked indifferent. When they panned to Chelsea, she held a pink fan to her lips and was smiling.

"Okay, we've all had enough preamble, haven't we?" Gareth called out. The men and women in the stands shouted in agreement.

"Well then, I see no reason to delay another moment. Let's begin!" he said and looked toward the large metal gate, which was closing shut.

Two large White Suits holding long swords in

front of them walked briskly from the gate toward where Rose and Delphine stood in the middle of the large stadium.

"Better get moving!" Gareth suggested to Rose and Delphine. One of the men approached Rose with his sword raised and thrust it at her leg, but she jumped away at the last moment. She looked back at him, surprised. As he stepped toward her again, Rose suddenly turned and rushed toward Delphine, swinging her weapon. Delphine easily blocked it with her own sword.

"Stop this!" I cried out into the emptiness of the room, wondering if anyone could hear me. No one responded and all I heard was the people yelling from the TV.

I saw just a flicker of fear in Delphine's eyes. Both girls stood still for a second. But then, each White Suit stomped forward again and both men, nearly simultaneously, jabbed their swords at the back of each girl's leg. Rose let out a high-pitched cry and reached down, grabbing the back of her leg. She had a gash across the fleshy part of her hamstring, just below her butt, and blood gushed through her hand's grip and ran down her calf.

Delphine appeared unscathed; she was able to dodge the oncoming sword. But she did look shocked, as if the immediacy of the situation finally registered. As Rose clasped at the back of her leg, Delphine charged forward and plunged her sword into the front of Rose's right thigh. Rose fell to her knees and looked at Delphine, who stood directly over her.

The cameramen didn't miss anything—they expertly switched from action shots of Rose and Delphine to extreme close-ups of Gareth and Chelsea's reactions, and then to the delighted faces of the spectators.

As Rose looked up at her attacker, Delphine lunged to grab the handle protruding from Rose. But Rose's hands moved from grasping the back of her leg to quickly pulling out the blade wedged deep in her thigh. As she yanked it out with one hard motion, blood sprayed out of the wound, and her cry rose up over the crowd's yells.

Before Delphine could react, Rose jumped up and charged at her opponent, flicking her wrist and jutting her arm forward forcefully, just like Ames had taught us. Her sword made contact just above Delphine's heart, nearly in the same spot Carl had pierced me. The tip of the blade just nicked Delphine and then fell to the ground, leaving each girl weaponless.

Blood pooled through Delphine's tank top and snaked down the front of her chest and legs onto the dirt. She cried out an angry, guttural scream, and without hesitation, lunged at Rose again, grabbing at her knees and pulling her down, both of their bodies hitting the ground with a thud amplified by the mics taped to their chests. The crowd let out a collective "ooh" and Gareth and Chelsea clapped in approval.

"This isn't okay!" I yelled out, but there was no

response. The only things I heard were grunts and cheers.

I watched helplessly as Rose and Delphine wrestled, punched, and kicked at each other, both trying to pull away to grab at one of the loose swords that were now just out of reach. Their faces were contorted in pain as they scratched at and tried to gouge each other's eyes. Rose yanked hard on Delphine's hair, and Delphine howled angrily. She bit Rose's shoulder hard in response, and blood spurt out of the corners of Delphine's mouth.

The crowd loved it—these two cute girls wrestling on the ground like this, their skin wet with sweat and blood. A group of men in the crowd taunted one another with fists of money waved in each other's faces. I realized there were bets on this match, and I wondered if that was the point of all this.

Delphine rolled away quickly, and as she reached down for one of the swords, Rose scrambled toward her and grabbed at her ankles, taking Delphine down hard onto the dirt. Delphine's face smacked the ground. The men and women in the stands screamed out, and as Delphine lifted herself up, Rose snatched the sword at her feet and jabbed it at Delphine's stomach, nicking her side as she rolled away to safety.

"You bitch!" Delphine yelled out. She stood back and grimaced, obviously in pain as blood streamed down her body. Gareth looked on, expressionless.

Rose, wild-eyed, grabbed the other sword and now charged back at Delphine with a weapon raised in each hand. Delphine, whose small size allowed her to duck out of trouble quickly, darted out of the way, and Rose spun around to face her opponent once again. I was surprised at her ferocity; it was something I'd never witnessed on the boat or in training.

Just then, the TV turned off.

"What? No!" I screamed out, and scrambled to grab the remote. I had to see what was going to happen. I snatched the remote, my hands trembling, and pressed the ON button again. The screen lit up again and I sighed audibly, relieved. I had to know if Delphine was going to be okay. And if she was, was she really going to kill Rose? The thought of either put my stomach in knots.

On the screen, Delphine looked fed up and angry. When Rose ran back at her, Delphine knelt down to the ground at the very last second, causing Rose to trip over her and launch through the air.

The sword in Rose's left hand went flying and landed with a thud several feet away, but the one gripped in her right hand swung upward, slicing into Rose's face as she fell. She writhed on the ground, holding her bloody cheek. When she moved her hand away, I saw a long gash where her skin was split open.

Delphine scrambled up, appearing unfazed by her own wounds, and picked up the sword that was now yards away from Rose. As Rose held her face, she glanced up at Delphine and tried to cower.

Pity flashed across Delphine's face for just a moment. Without another second of hesitation, she plunged her sword downward into Rose's chest. I flinched, instantly reminded again of what I did to Carl.

Rose's body shuddered for a moment and then went still. Delphine collapsed on the ground next to her, clutching at the cut on her side. In close-up, I saw the wound was deep. Delphine's face was turning pale as a wet blanket of blood spread out on the ground around her.

CHAPTER 2

"Someone help her! Please!" I called out again. Moments later, two White Suits carrying a stretcher emerged from the metal gates and ran over, lifting Delphine onto the canvas material and carting her away quickly.

The men and women in the crowd stood up as she was hauled out of the stadium, applauding Delphine like she was an injured football player.

As the camera moved across the people, I spotted Titus. It *had* to be him.

I recognized that tanned face, his white teeth clenched in a wide, extreme smile. This guy was wearing sunglasses, so I couldn't be one hundred percent sure, but his demeanor and attitude looked so similar, cheering and laughing with a man to his left that I didn't recognize.

"It's him!" I screamed out, not expecting any response.

Gareth stood up, his arm around Chelsea who beamed with a wide and brilliant smile, like a princess holding court.

"What an impressive debut match!" he said, and the men and women in the crowd yelled out their approval.

"Delphine's something else, isn't she? Don't worry, you'll be seeing more of her soon enough. We'll make sure she's healed nice and quick so we can all get another look at her," he said. "Don't fret about her, my friends. I'm going to take *very* good care of this girl," he continued, with a hint of innuendo that could only mean one thing, and the people in the crowd laughed.

"Now, time to move on. Are you all ready

for the main event?" he asked, and everyone applauded.

The main event? So, Delphine and Rose's match was just a warm-up to something bigger? I was disgusted that our lives meant so little.

As the gate slowly began to rise, my door also opened and a White Suit walked in. He promptly unplugged my TV from the wall and lifted it into his arms.

"Wait! What are you doing?" I stood up and faced him angrily. "I was watching that!"

"Not anymore," the White Suit responded as he began to move toward the door, taking the TV with him.

"Why not?"

"Doctor's orders," he said and disappeared as quickly as he had come in.

I stumbled over to the exit and pulled at the door's metal handle, but I was locked in. I was annoyed that I hadn't acted in that moment and attacked him, and at least tried to escape this room. It had all happened too quickly.

I collapsed to the ground and leaned against the door. It was all sinking in. I felt like an idiot for thinking that when we first arrived this place might be part of some test of the Ship Out program.

Today, the truth felt very bleak. Not only was I probably going to die on this island—eventually, if not right away—everyone else from the boat was going to die here too, if they hadn't already.

But Ames and Elise had talked about escape, so I needed to get them alone to hear what they were thinking. Chelsea also seemed like she'd help me leave, but her connection to Gareth now made me question everything she said, and I felt Elise and Ames were my best hope to have a shot of getting out of here.

As I sat there, with no idea of what to do next or how to reach them, I thought about killing Carl again. Just like I wasn't able to help my brother

James, I couldn't help Carl, either. I felt angry that I was forced to murder Carl just so I could live.

I wondered why the spectators enjoyed watching people die. I guessed that maybe seeing teenagers literally fight for their lives gave the visitors a rush they couldn't find in any legal way back home. Ames had alluded to it himself—this island was all about illicit thrills that couldn't be found anywhere else.

Praeclarus couldn't be a large group. From my own experience in the Coliseum and watching Delphine's fight, I gathered there were around forty people in the crowd who weren't White Suits, prostitutes or other island staff. Gareth undoubtedly needed to be very careful who he let come here and who he let leave. I had so many questions about who these people were, where we were, and how I got here.

I knew Ames and Elise thought they needed my help—or more precisely, my dad's help, but I had no idea how to reach him. Hopefully they'd already figured out that part. But if anyone had the means to get us out of here, I realized my dad might be one in a million. We just needed to get him the message that I was in trouble.

My bandages were soaked through with blood and I knew Elise would be here soon to tend to me. I moved to the couch and waited for her to walk through the door. We'd have to come up with a plan before I was healed and forced to fight again.

Hours later, my door clicked open and I turned expectantly, anxious for the opportunity to finally talk to Elise again. Instead, I saw Darby enter the room.

"Where's Elise?" I demanded.

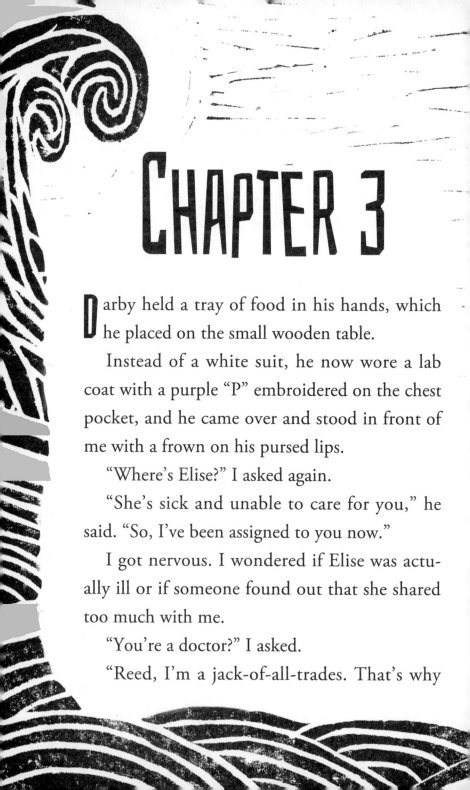

CHAPTER 3

Darby held a tray of food in his hands, which he placed on the small wooden table.

Instead of a white suit, he now wore a lab coat with a purple "P" embroidered on the chest pocket, and he came over and stood in front of me with a frown on his pursed lips.

"Where's Elise?" I asked again.

"She's sick and unable to care for you," he said. "So, I've been assigned to you now."

I got nervous. I wondered if Elise was actually ill or if someone found out that she shared too much with me.

"You're a doctor?" I asked.

"Reed, I'm a jack-of-all-trades. That's why

they keep me around," he said as he peeled off my old bandage from my shoulder. I cringed from the pain as he tugged at the gauze, which had adhered to the wound.

"What is wrong with Elise, exactly? Will she back soon?"

"Why are you so interested in Elise?" he asked, looking down at me over his wire-rimmed glasses. I had to be careful. Did he know that Elise had said something to me? And what about Ames?

"I'm not," I stammered, looking away.

"Your wounds are healing nicely," he said as he applied new bandages to my leg. "You'll be out of here soon enough. Gareth will be happy. You made quite an impression in your first battle."

"Am I going to have to fight again?"

"Yes, of course," he responded matter-of-factly, like I had asked if the sky was blue. "Now, I'm sure you're hungry by now. Eat up to help regain your strength. I'll be back tomorrow to check on you again," he said before quickly exiting. He was

all business now, no longer the friendly and warm host he'd been when we first arrived at the island. I heard the door lock behind him.

I was starving and I ate the dinner of steak, buttered vegetables, and seeded bread quickly. Soon, I felt a little bit better. As I finished, I heard the door open again and I swung around to see who it was.

Chelsea stood at the door, leaning against the frame. "Hello there, friend," she said, smiling. The strap of her dress fell off her shoulder just so, as if she'd planned it that way.

She strode across the room and sat next to me on the bed. She tilted her head and stared at me for a long time. I tried not to feel embarrassed or intimidated as she continued to look at me, or when she traced my bandages with just the tips of her fingers. "Are you feeling any better?" she finally asked.

"I'm okay." I tried to sound normal, but winced

as I sat up in bed. "What are you doing here again? Don't you have someone else to mess with?"

I didn't trust her—especially seeing her applaud Delphine and Rose's fight—but as I said this, Chelsea looked hurt.

"Listen, when you first came to the island, I took an interest in you because you're my type," she said.

I felt myself blush immediately. I tried to change the subject to what I really wanted to know about. "When we talked before, you said you were putting together a plan to get out of here. What did you mean?"

"Before we talk about that, I want to get to know you, Reed. I need to know I can trust you first. But you're just so hot, it's distracting me," she said, leaning into me and resting her hand on my leg.

This flirting excited me, which annoyed me. I was fairly certain that her sweet talk was some sort of mind game, and that I was dumb to be flattered by her advances.

"I've been here so long, I get really bored and lonely, so anyone new that shows up and is *actually* cute and not a fat, perverted old man, well, that's exciting to me, Reed," Chelsea continued, twisting the corner of her lips into a small but suggestive smile.

"Aren't you pleased that you're the one that interests me?" she asked, like she was accusing me of something. I was pretty sure that I was being played.

"I don't know if you're telling the truth. I think you enjoy messing with me," I responded, pulling away from her as she leaned further into me, smelling sweet.

"Why would I do that?" she asked, wide eyed. She looked hurt by the accusation.

"Because you're bored," I said in return, and she laughed, insistently pressing her body into me. Her long dark hair fell over her shoulders and brushed against my arm. I felt a jolt run through my body all the way to my toes, and I could tell I was turning red. Girls never made me feel this nervous.

"Reed, I've been on this island for way too long. I can't help but be curious, even if I'm supposed to stay away."

"So, you shouldn't be here? You're going to get us both in trouble."

"Yes and no. You see, I'd get my wrist slapped at worst if anyone found out. My dad doesn't want me *actually* talking to anyone on the island. He likes to show me off to his friends, but he doesn't want me to have any friends of my own. So I get restless with nobody to talk to and no one to touch," she said, moving her hand further up my thigh. Despite my best intentions, I didn't pull away.

"Don't worry, Reed. I have my dad wrapped around this finger." She held up her pinky and wagged it at me.

"So . . . you mentioned you can help me

escape?" I asked, trying to circle back to what I really needed to know about.

"Shh . . . we'll get to that," she said, putting her finger to my lips as if to silence me. I pushed it away.

"Where's Elise?" I asked. As intrigued by Chelsea as I was, I needed to figure out how to get off the island as soon as possible. Chelsea shrugged, pulling her hand away from me and seeming annoyed at my persistent change in subject.

"I haven't see her in a few days. Why do you care?"

I hesitated for a moment, trying to figure out if I was about to say too much or if Chelsea could actually help me too. I didn't think I could trust her, but as we sat together, she looked at me so earnestly.

"Elise says that she needs me to help get her off the island," I blurted out and immediately regretted it. Chelsea raised her eyebrows and laughed to herself.

"Oh, really? That *is* interesting." I couldn't tell if she was calculating something in her mind as a long pause stretched out between us. I was about to mention Ames as well, but thought better of it, as Chelsea wasn't as receptive as I had hoped.

"No offense, but why does Elise need you?" Chelsea finally asked.

"Oh, I don't know," I said, but my voice cracked.

"Reed, are you telling me the truth?" she asked, looking at me with those big brown eyes. Her gaze felt like some sort of inescapable mind control. I was suddenly compelled to tell her everything.

"Well, I think it's because of my dad. If I can communicate with him, he has the means to find us and to help us get out of here."

She smirked, but didn't say anything, and instead sat staring at me with a dark look on her face and then abruptly said, "Tell me about where you're from."

"Wait . . . what? I don't want to talk about

that," I responded. "Can you help us get out of here or not?"

She sighed loudly, obviously annoyed. "I'll be honest. It's going to be hard to leave this place, but it's true that I'm coming up with a solid plan and you need to be patient. Anyone who has ever tried to escape? Well, it hasn't ended well for them so we have to be careful. Anyway . . . I don't really want to talk about that right now. I want to talk about you. Won't you please tell me about where you're from?" she repeated. She then leaned over, rested her head in my lap and lay in the bed beside me, her legs curled up beside mine. It felt intimate and I was both excited and nervous by how comfortable she was with me already. *What's the harm in opening up a little bit*, I wondered. I wanted her to trust me—to side with me.

"I'm from a suburb outside Portland, Oregon," I said.

"Where's Oregon? That's part of the United States, right? And what's a suburb?" she asked.

I was surprised she didn't know these things. I laughed and her face turned red immediately. It was the first time I'd seen her flustered.

"Oh, I'm sorry! I thought you were messing with me," I responded, and couldn't help myself but reach down and twirl a strand of her hair between my fingers.

I wondered where she was from. She spoke with an unreadable accent—almost American, almost English, almost Australian. I couldn't be sure.

"Can you tell me about Oregon? Is it nice?" she asked, looking up at me with those big, shiny eyes. It was so earnest, I couldn't help but find her charming.

"It's alright—there are lots of trees and it rains pretty much nonstop in the winter. There's not much to do there if you're not into hiking and boating and stuff like that," I continued. "But, given the circumstances, I'd kill to be back home right now," I said.

She laughed. "That's a funny choice of words, Reed."

I hadn't meant it like that.

"Now it's my turn to ask you a question," I said.

Chelsea nodded. "Fair enough."

I had about a thousand questions but one kept rising to the top of the pile in my mind as I tried to piece everything together about what I knew so far.

"Who are the members of Praeclarus? I don't understand who'd *want* to watch kids kill each other."

Chelsea thought this was hilarious and laughed to herself. Finally, she calmed down and looked right at me.

"There are a lot of sick people in this world, Reed. That's what growing up here has taught me more than anything."

I waited for more elaboration, but Chelsea grew quiet.

"But who are they?"

She sighed and shrugged, then started talking again.

"They're a select group of rich assholes that belong to a very, very exclusive club. No one in the 'real world' knows Praeclarus exists. It's a group that my dad and his buddies have been in for years. The island is my dad's way to treat these friends to very special vacations," Chelsea explained. "The type of vacations that you can't have in the 'real world.' Most Praeclarus members come here multiple times a year," she continued. "They're a chain, all these people; they're all intimately connected. If one link breaks, then everyone is in trouble. They're all complicit. Everyone's in too deep to change course now, to make amends for the sins they witness here. Actually, not only witness, but participate in. Joining Praeclarus is kind of like selling your soul."

"So . . . how many people are in Praeclarus?"

"Maybe around fifty or sixty?"

I couldn't believe there were so many people

in the world that would choose to watch people murder each other.

"But why?"

"Idle time? I know boredom, and it can drive a person to do things you wouldn't believe," Chelsea said.

I sighed, trying to process what she was telling me. It sounded crazy. My dad was a blowhard, but at least he was trying to do good things with his power and fame.

Chelsea continued. "My dad basically set this island up to show off and to wield power over his friends. He created a place where you can do anything, see anything, feel anything you want, and your secrets are safe."

"Why are you telling me all this?" I asked. I felt confused by Chelsea's intentions. During the fights, she stood next to Gareth, cheering on the bloodshed like everyone else. I pointed this out.

"I *have* to, Reed. My dad threatens me with all sorts of awful things if I don't look the part and smile and pretend to love every minute of what happens here."

"How long have you been on the island?" I asked.

"My whole life," she replied and my stomach dropped.

It's been that long?

We heard footsteps and muffled voices coming down the hallway and Chelsea went silent, putting her finger up to my lips to silence me. Despite what she said, I sensed we'd be in huge trouble if we were found together like this. The steps grew more and more distant and finally disappeared before I started talking again.

"Your whole life? This place has existed that long?"

"Oh yeah, but the fighting thing only started a few years ago," Chelsea said. "I think my dad was getting bored himself."

Delphine suddenly flashed into my mind. "Can

you tell me about Delphine? Is she okay? And what about Micah? Where is he?"

"Enough, enough."

Chelsea waved off these questions, annoyed.

"Now it's my turn to ask you something else," she said, sitting up and twisting her body to lean into me. Her face was now just inches from mine. I pulled back nervously.

"Do you like me?" she asked, with a serious look on her face.

"Yeah, you seem alright," I said, trying to play it cool.

"Oh, wow, thanks, Reed," she responded sarcastically and then rested her shoulder against my chest. Her hair fell over her front and tickled my bare arm.

"But do you really like me?" she tilted her head up and now her lips were so very close. I didn't know how to respond, and hesitated. It was obviously she enjoyed toying with people.

"Oh, come on, Reed. Lighten up and give me a

kiss," she said, and instead of letting me respond, she shifted all of her weight onto me and pressed her lips against mine. I tensed up for a moment and then relaxed, kissing her back.

For just a split second, I forgot where I was and felt a rush of adrenaline speed through me. I couldn't believe I was with such a beautiful girl. My friends at home would be impressed. But then I realized that she'd be able to leave this cell and wouldn't ever face death in the Coliseum, and I'd stay behind and eventually be forced to fight again. I felt angry and I pulled away from her kiss abruptly.

"Why are you upset?" she asked, looking at me confused.

"Because this is all just a distraction. I need to figure out a way out of here," I said. I paused, thinking everything through.

"You should come with us—with the plan Elise is putting together—you'd just need to join in," I suggested. She had been here her whole life—she knew no other reality than this place. I knew she deserved a happier life than this. And more people working together on a unified plan to escape was better, right? It had to be.

Chelsea didn't respond, and I hoped she was taking the offer seriously. Even though in my heart I knew it was foolish, I was starting to have feelings for her.

"So, do you think it is possible . . . to leave this place?" I asked.

"Anything's possible, but no one's ever succeeded," she said. "That's why you can't rush and you need to think everything through. I am working on something too, but we can't be too rash. You gotta be careful, Reed."

"So, how many people have tried to escape?"

"Many, actually."

"What happened to them?"

"Well, my dad doesn't take well to people trying to leave. It always causes quite a scene. Inevitably, he comes up with new and spectacular ways to punish and kill each offender—and everyone is forced to watch, even the visitors. This helps to ensure that no one has loose lips when they're back home."

I nodded my head, thinking.

"How did you get in here?" I asked.

"There are key pads at every entrance and I cracked the code, so to speak," she said. "It was actually super easy. Just had to befriend the right person. I usually can get my way if I set my mind to something," she said, looking me straight in the eye. Given her looks and gifts of persuasion, I was pretty certain she flirted with the right guard to figure out a way inside to flirt with me.

"So now I can move freely among rooms. As long as the wrong White Suit doesn't spot me entering somewhere I'm not supposed to be, I'm all good."

"And how did you enter my room? Aren't the Suits stationed outside all day?"

"Well, I'm selective about when I try to come

see you. And, I have a way with all of those guys anyway."

I had a feeling she had a way with most people she interacted with.

"Anyway, I should go before it gets too late," she said. She moved her head in again and gave me a long, hard kiss and then stood up and went to the door.

"Join our plan," I suggested again, but she didn't respond.

As she was leaving, she turned around to look at me. "I'll try to come see you again as soon as I can."

Before I could ask her anything more, she was out the door and it clicked shut. As I sat there, I recounted the whole conversation in my head. She was so beautiful; I couldn't wait to see her again.

Now, I had to shake her from my brain so I could think clearly. I knew just a little bit more about Praeclarus now. I was disturbed that there were so many of them out there, living in the world as upstanding, rich citizens, but secretly co-conspirators to murder for entertainment.

I wanted to know what others trapped on the island had done to try to escape.

I sat thinking about everything for a long time until I began to grow sleepy, so I turned over in bed, trying to get comfortable. I was completely exhausted in every possible way. Despite this, I tossed and turned all night, thinking about my parents. Did they know we were missing yet? I think we weren't expected back home for a few days, but I was getting confused about time being locked up inside without daylight and darkness to guide me.

When we didn't return to the port in San Diego as expected, I was sure my dad would immediately send numerous search planes crisscrossing the ocean to track us down. But did he have any idea where the Ship Out boat had headed in the first place? And did Titus take us on a completely different route to bring us here?

Although my dad and I didn't get along great, I took comfort in thinking about airplanes roving over the ocean waters searching for us—if not today, they'd be deployed very soon. Using all of his wealth and resources, he'd find us. I had to believe that to be true.

CHAPTER 4

I was in the apartment prison cell for many more days, although I'm not sure how many exactly. There was no sunlight in the room and no clock.

I tried to keep track of the time based on the type of food a White Suit brought me. After each meal I assumed to be dinner, I'd attempt to fall asleep and inevitably toss and turn until breakfast was brought in.

Darby visited often to check on me, but never said much, even when I attempted to strike up conversation. He scribbled notes into a leather-bound book and then promptly went away. I felt like his previous kind nature when we arrived on the island had been a lie to lull us into trusting him and not asking too many questions.

I waited for Chelsea to come back, but she never returned. I turned over possible scenarios again and again, driving myself crazy. Maybe she had been found out and she was in trouble? Maybe she was already bored with me? Maybe she was kissing someone else?

I knew my jealous thoughts were ridiculous, given my circumstances. I shouldn't even be thinking about a girl, but I couldn't help but fantasize about her kiss and the weight of her warm body against me.

To pass the time, I practiced a familiar mental exercise again and again by trying to catalog every memory I had of my brother, James. Things that I could actually remember us doing together, not stories my parents had told me after his death.

I did this exercise every couple of months since his death—it was a mental inventory of James and me:

1. Catching fish off the dock at our summer house
2. Sliding down our staircase on a sled of pillows
3. Camping in our living room with a tent made of sheets strung between furniture
4. Skipping smooth, round rocks at the lake
5. Sneaking out of our house to walk around our neighborhood at night

The list started at sixty-two memories immediately following his death. That number shrunk by a few every couple of months.

Today, as I recounted everything, the number was at twenty-six. I was forgetting the small details about James, and although I remembered what he looked like, the image in my head was becoming fuzzy around the edges.

I sat down against the cold concrete wall and couldn't help but cry. I was overwhelmed by a new sadness that hadn't been there before. I hadn't said a proper goodbye to my parents. I turned my back on my mom when she tried to hug me as I boarded *The Last Chance*. The irony of the boat name wasn't lost on me. I wondered where my mom was at this very moment. Did she think that I was lost at sea? And if I died here, how many memories would she have of me?

I felt sorry for myself, sitting there, trapped. And then I was mad for feeling sorry for myself; it was so pitiful. I didn't have any idea how to get out of there on my own. The way Elise and Ames made it seem, my best hope was my dad and his resources, and that he'd figure out where we were and help us. I'd been nothing but a shit to him for the previous two years, and suddenly he was the key to my freedom.

I heard the door open and I looked up. Chelsea was standing there, looking down at me, unamused.

She glared and hissed, "Geez—what is wrong with you?"

Embarrassed, I wiped at the tears that streaked down my cheeks.

"Nothing. I'm fine," I replied, but I'm sure I didn't sound very convincing.

"Well, get up." She offered her hand to help lift me up and I accepted it. Her grip was warm, and as I stood up, she peered into my eyes. "You look terrible."

"Yeah, thanks."

"Well, I'm here to cheer you up. When was the last time Darby was here?"

"About two hours ago?" I guessed, although maybe it had just been thirty minutes. Time was weird and amorphous when you had no activities or light to help measure things.

"And I see you ate dinner already. You weren't hungry?" she asked as she looked over at my plate with my half-eaten burger.

"Not really," I responded.

"And how are your shoulder and leg? Doing better?"

"Getting there, yeah," I said. I was feeling much

better physically. It was just my head now that was messed up.

"Good. Then, here . . . " She handed over a black duffel bag to me.

"What is this?"

"An early Christmas present. Open it up and see," Chelsea said.

I unzipped the bag and saw white clothing folded neatly inside. I pulled out the item on the top and saw that it was a jacket. A pair of pants was beneath that. And a white bowler hat was tucked to the side.

I looked at her surprised. "Is this what I think it is?"

"Yes, of course. Now put it on. I want to take you somewhere and this will make things much easier."

"Isn't someone watching us now?" I looked up at the camera that was pointing down from the ceiling.

"Yes, but it's a good friend, if you know what

I mean," she said winking at me, and I couldn't tell if she was joking. "C'mon. We have nothing to worry about as long as we're back before sunrise," she said.

Although I didn't quite trust her, I wanted to believe Chelsea wouldn't screw me over outright. And, besides, nothing good was coming from me being trapped in this room. Maybe out there I could figure out a way to escape on my own.

"Okay. Okay. Where are you taking me?"

"Reed! You have to trust me. You think I'd want to hurt you?"

"No, of course not," I stammered, not wanting her to change her mind about whatever plan she had.

I was about to take off my shirt, but felt embarrassed by Chelsea standing there, watching me.

"Oh please, Reed, I've seen it all before. Now get dressed so we don't lose any more time," she ordered, and I changed into the suit as she watched me, smiling with a mischievous look in her eye.

"Well, you certainly look the part," Chelsea said when I was finished, appraising my outfit. "Now, let's go." She took my hand and opened the door. "Walk directly behind me and appear confident. Don't make eye contact with anyone we pass. Only look straight ahead. It's very late, so we won't run into too many people, but we can never be too careful, okay?"

"Yes," I responded as we entered a dim, yellowed hallway. Stark white tiles covered the flooring and there were no windows. No one else was around.

Chelsea walked at a brisk pace and I struggled to keep up as we turned corners, going from one long, dark hallway to the next again and again. I didn't dare speak because I didn't want to draw attention to myself. We passed many doors, each with its own keypad entry, and I wondered what was on the other side of each one—Praeclarus members? Staff? More prisoners? How many of us were there? I had heard distant cheers the past couple of days, so I assumed there were more fights taking place.

We continued walking through the labyrinth of hallways and suddenly I heard footsteps clacking down the hall far away. A White Suit turned the corner and was walking quickly toward us. My heart started pounding furiously. Crap. This was it. He'd definitely know it was me. I remembered what Chelsea said about looking ahead and tried my best to appear normal.

"Hi, Raj," Chelsea called out as the man got closer. "What a wonderful surprise to run into you!"

"Hi, Chelsea! You're out late tonight," the person responded as we walked passed him. I snuck a glance sideways and I saw him smiling widely at Chelsea, not even noticing me. She was like a shooting star—you couldn't help but stare.

We never slowed as we passed him, and Chelsea called out over her shoulder, "Always a pleasure to see you, Raj," as we left him behind us.

"You know the pleasure is all mine, Chelsea," he said back. It was obvious to me he was trying to flirt.

"See? You have nothing to worry about," Chelsea muttered under her breath, and I relaxed slightly.

We came upon a tall, red door with a keypad. I hadn't been here yet.

"Bend down and pretend you're tying your shoelace, and don't look up," Chelsea ordered. I did what she commanded. While I was pretending to fumble with the lace, she punched in the code and the door swung open.

"C'mon," Chelsea said and we walked through the door onto a path. It was lined with large, thick trees that were aglow from light posts that dotted a trail snaking up a hillside. I didn't see anyone else and our pace slowed slightly.

"Where are we?" I asked.

"Patience, my friend. You wanted to see the island, right?" she asked, grabbing my hand and pulling me along. "And don't even think about trying to escape," she warned. "That would be very foolish. You gotta stick with me, okay?"

"Okay," I agreed, but still felt uncertain about whether I could actually trust her.

The path was smooth dirt and we walked along it for several minutes, not speaking. We were going up in elevation so rapidly, the moon appeared as though it was getting closer. Chelsea looked back on occasion to smile at me, her face glowing under the pearly light.

The air was brisk and quiet. I didn't hear anything except for our breathing as the path got even steeper and more challenging. Finally, we reached a little viewpoint cut into the hillside that was lined with ornately carved wooden benches.

"Check this out," Chelsea said as she stood on one of the benches and reached out her hand to pull me up. I stepped up and looked out at the view of everything that lay in the valley beneath us.

From this vantage point we looked down at

almost the entire island, and in the distance the ocean sparkled under the moon's light. There was no other land in the distance.

"Isn't it beautiful?" Chelsea asked as we stared down at the scene below. To the left, I saw the Coliseum. In the blue glow of the night sky, its white marble ring reminded me of a skeletal jaw, opened wide.

"No, I don't think it's beautiful at all," I responded, thinking about Delphine, Rose, and Carl, and the countless strangers that had probably been thrown into battle against their will.

"Well, I know what happens down there is terrible, but from up here, it almost doesn't look real. I like being up here, removed from everything," Chelsea said, leaning her head on my shoulder.

"See that large building over there?" she asked, pointing to a big structure that was lit up like a neon sign. Even from far away, the building conveyed importance. It appeared to be crafted out of tall marble columns, and was aglow with glittery, yellow lights.

"Yeah, what is that?"

"That's the hotel for our guests here," Chelsea said. "I've been told it's nicer than any five-star resort anywhere in the world," she continued. "Plus, there are all the other perks, if you know what I mean," she joked.

"Prostitution?" I asked, even though I was nearly certain the answer.

"Well, that's not what my dad calls it, but yes, and that's just the start."

"That's disgusting," I said.

"Yeah, but that's one of the island's most popular attractions. The men come here thinking there are no strings attached, but really, they're tightly intertwined with my dad and this place forever."

"So who are all the staff here? Where do they come from? And why do they cooperate?" I asked.

"Most come voluntarily. My dad offers Suits a fresh start. There are a lot of people just waiting for the chance to run away. And as long as they don't act up, he treats them very, very well. The one caveat is that they can never ever leave, and they can never try to make contact with anyone from their previous lives," Chelsea explained.

"And where does Elise stay?" I asked.

She looked at me and narrowed her eyes, but then pointed to a smaller, more plain-looking building near the Coliseum. "All the staff live there."

I grew quiet, staring out at the land and trying to take it all in, to memorize it. I spotted various ugly, simple buildings that looked like bunkers, and I guessed that might be where the prisoners stayed. In the distance, a tall marble building with a courtyard stood out and I recognized it as the training grounds Darby brought us to when we first arrived.

I couldn't see the beaches very well from this viewing point, but there looked to be a few docks lining the water, and one that appeared to be a landing pad for helicopters.

Then, in the distance—I spotted one gigantic building. It was much bigger than any other structure. It seemed to be windowless, but its long expanse of metallic roof caught the moon's light.

"What's that?" I asked, pointing to the building.

"That's my dad's airplane hangar. It's actually the one building on the entire island I can't access—or even get near—so I don't know for sure what happens there. I have my suspicions, but my dad absolutely refuses to share anything with me about it. I've tried to get there on my own, but my gifts of persuasion don't work with the guards over there, unfortunately."

We were quiet for a few moments, and I thought about everything she told me.

"So, this is what you wanted to show me?" I asked. I wasn't sure how seeing all of this was going to help me escape.

"Well, this is just one stop. Let's keep moving,"

Chelsea said as she stepped down from the bench and moved back onto the path. I hopped off to catch up as she headed downhill quickly onto the other side of the mountain, away from where we had come.

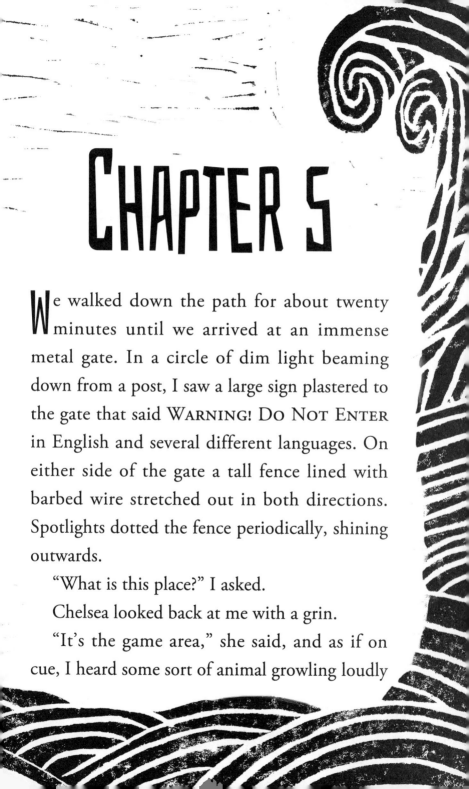

CHAPTER 5

We walked down the path for about twenty minutes until we arrived at an immense metal gate. In a circle of dim light beaming down from a post, I saw a large sign plastered to the gate that said WARNING! DO NOT ENTER in English and several different languages. On either side of the gate a tall fence lined with barbed wire stretched out in both directions. Spotlights dotted the fence periodically, shining outwards.

"What is this place?" I asked.

Chelsea looked back at me with a grin.

"It's the game area," she said, and as if on cue, I heard some sort of animal growling loudly on the other side of the fence, sounding as though it was just feet away from us. I jumped back, startled, and looked toward the noise. In the darkness, two yellow eyes glinted on the other side.

"What the hell is that?" I hissed at her, taking more steps backwards.

"It's a tiger," she said, like it was no big deal. Shining her flashlight at the animal revealed the tiger's orange and black fur. "I call him Oliver. He's so beautiful, isn't he?" she asked, reaching her hand out and touching the fence. "He's new, actually."

"Where did he come from?"

"I don't know," Chelsea responded. "My dad gets them shipped in. But I have no idea where they originate."

"They? There's more than one?"

"Yeah, come with me," Chelsea said and continued to walk along the fence. It extended out as far as my eyes could see before being engulfed in darkness on both sides. We walked quickly and I heard bushes and grass moving on the other side of the fence as we continued. I wondered if the tiger was following us, and I felt uneasy.

After a few minutes, she stopped again. "Look in there," she ordered, pointing her flashlight at a different enclosure.

I didn't want to get too close, but stepped forward to look in and saw a bear curled up in a ball, sleeping.

"Is that what I think it is?"

"Yep," she said.

"Why are these animals here? What is this place?"

"Hunting grounds. It's illegal to kill these animals in a lot of places, but here . . . "

"Anything goes?" I said, finishing her sentence.

"You're catching on," she said.

I felt glum, as the island just got worse and worse the more I learned about it.

"What happens to the animals after they are killed?" I asked.

"Well, the bodies aren't allowed to leave the island. It's too risky for my dad. People would definitely start asking questions if they spotted a stuffed tiger displayed in someone's house, right?"

"So they're killed for nothing?"

"No, not exactly. Remember the hotel? Well, there's a big dining room in there. That's where the animals are displayed. It's a popular source of bragging rights among the members. The guy who has the biggest, fiercest animal on display also has the biggest, fiercest—you know . . . "

She looked at me and winked and I rolled my eyes, which made her laugh. She grabbed my hand and suddenly yanked me down to the ground before kissing me hard and long, and again, I didn't stop her, even though I knew I probably should. Didn't Elise say she was with someone else? Who?

She pulled away and was quiet, staring up at the sky.

"I like to come here in the middle of the night.

It's peaceful and the animals don't act scared. Especially the new ones." she said. "They don't know what's coming."

I couldn't tell if that delighted or repulsed her. I noticed the sky was turning a muddy brown, and I knew that the sun would be rising soon.

"Shouldn't we get back?" I asked. I was worried about being discovered. I thought with or without Chelsea, if I was spotted outside my room, I'd be killed straight away.

"Awww, Reed. You're so paranoid. Yes, I suppose," she hopped up and we headed back up the path then over the mountain. We were quiet as we walked, and as we went over the top of the hill, I saw the whole Praeclarus compound stretched out like a glittery claw beneath us.

I didn't want to return and wished there was a way to escape in that moment. I briefly contemplated taking Chelsea hostage. What if I brought her to Gareth and threatened to kill her if he didn't let me go?

Chelsea looked at me and smiled, and I immediately felt guilty for considering it.

"So, what's your plan to get out of here? Can't you tell me?" I asked her.

"Be quiet, we're almost there."

As we passed another White Suit on the path, he looked me straight in the eye. For a split second, I spotted an expression of recognition on his face, and Chelsea glared at him.

"Everything okay, Samson?"

There was a long pause and I contemplated running then—I was pretty fast, but I had no idea where to go.

"Yes, Chelsea. Everything is A-Okay. Just surprised you are out so early in the morning, that's all," he said, and hurried away, not looking at me again. I had no idea if he knew who I was and hoped I could get back to my room before someone else found me out.

As we got back to my door, I couldn't help but

feel relieved as we entered my "apartment," which was really a glorified prison cell.

"So, what's next?" I asked, still not sure if she wanted to join us in trying to put together a plan to get out of there.

"Don't worry, Reed. You'll see me around," she said and gave me one quick peck. And with that, she was gone again.

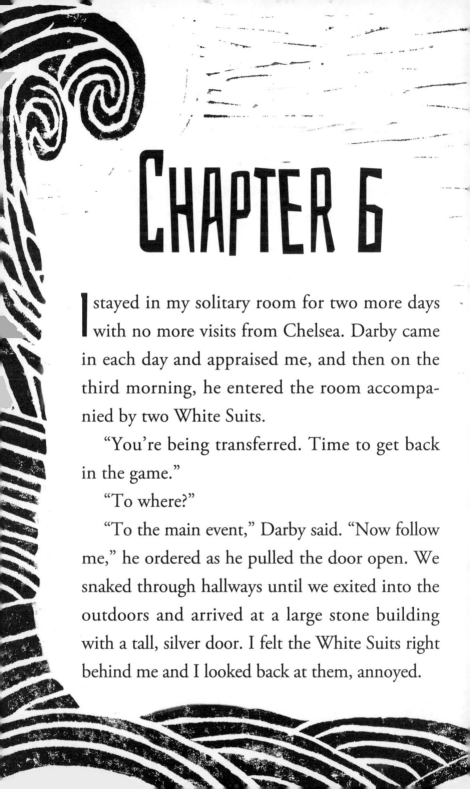

CHAPTER 6

I stayed in my solitary room for two more days with no more visits from Chelsea. Darby came in each day and appraised me, and then on the third morning, he entered the room accompanied by two White Suits.

"You're being transferred. Time to get back in the game."

"To where?"

"To the main event," Darby said. "Now follow me," he ordered as he pulled the door open. We snaked through hallways until we exited into the outdoors and arrived at a large stone building with a tall, silver door. I felt the White Suits right behind me and I looked back at them, annoyed.

"Don't worry, I'm not going anywhere. Where could I go, anyway?"

The door slid open as a White Suit prodded me in the back with a baton. I walked forward, uncertain of what I was about to face.

I was now in a big dirt courtyard, similar to the training area Darby originally brought us to the day we left the boat, but much bigger. There was a large group of kids standing there, huddled around a drinking fountain, and they all turned to stare at me. I quickly scanned the group—it was about thirty kids around my age, mostly guys, and I didn't recognize any of them.

"Fresh meat!" a giant kid with an Irish or English accent called out and everyone laughed. A few others yelled at me in languages of unknown origin, and I couldn't help but lower my gaze. Knowing that showing any weakness would likely make me a target, I forced myself to stand upright, raise my head again, and try to look cocky, which

was pretty much the exact opposite of how I felt inside.

The kids were all muscular and tanned, and they were obviously in the middle of some sort of strenuous workout, as they appeared sweaty and winded.

I spotted Ames standing to the side of the group and I tried to catch his eye, but he wouldn't look at me directly as everyone continued to yell at me and call me names.

"Meat!"

"Dead man walking!"

"Pussy!"

"Calm down, calm down . . ." Darby called out to everyone, and the group quieted and looked at him, annoyed but obedient.

"Everybody, this is Reed," he said, pushing me forward toward the group. "He's a decent enough fighter to make it to the Main Event. He got a little nicked up last battle, but now he's okay. Right, Reed?"

"Yes, I'm fine," I responded, glaring back at the group, and trying to appear cooler than I felt.

"Reed!" a voice called out and I saw Delphine push through the huddle of boys standing before her. She was wearing a sports bra, and her shoulder and side were both covered in large, white bandages, but otherwise, she looked better than I expected. She smiled at me and I grinned back at her, thrilled she was alive and looked okay, all things considered. Everyone turned to stare at her, and parted so she could move forward toward me.

"Delphine. Why are you here? Where are we?" I was confused. I wanted to know who these kids were and what happened to everyone from the boat.

"Well, Reed, you've made it to the big time." Darby chimed in. "Just think, if you hadn't shown any promise during entrant training, you could've been delegated as a Suit instead, but Gareth thought you were worthy enough to enter the real fighters' program. Congratulations. Now don't squander this opportunity," Darby said, first looking at me, and then turning to address everyone.

"Remember, you're all only a handful of wins away from freedom. Ten wins—that is it—your ticket out of here with millions in an offshore bank account," he continued. "It's not that bad given the payoff. Now, get back to work," Darby said and then exited through the large gate again, with a group of White Suits close behind.

"Welcome, Reed. I knew I'd see you again," Ames said as he walked over to me and shook my hand firmly, holding my eye contact. I read in his eyes and the long pause that he wasn't going to address our previous conversations with everyone else around. I'd have to figure out a way to get him alone so we could really talk.

"Now, let's get to it. Odin—come over here, I want you to meet Reed," Ames said, calling back to a large kid with olive skin and pale yellow-green eyes. It was the dude with the accent who called me "fresh meat." He walked over, looking me up and down slowly as if sizing me up.

"Reed's your new training partner, okay?" Ames asked, but it really wasn't a question. Odin sighed, obviously annoyed.

"Really? This newbie? Give me a break, Ames," Odin looked at me dismissively.

"Oh, I think you can both teach each other a lot. But really, you're a good size match-up. I bet you'll find Reed to be quite a challenge," Ames said, winking at Odin. "Now, go ahead . . . "

Before I could react, Odin charged at me and lifted me off of the ground, tossing me down like a sack of potatoes. Everyone else watching us laughed and I felt my face turn red. As I stumbled to get back up, Delphine stared at me with her squinty, pretty eyes and gave me a look like she wished there was something she could do to help. I brushed off the dirt from my clothes, and started to walk away from Odin, rather than give him the satisfaction of reacting angrily and pushing back.

As I moved away from him, I felt a hard shove against my back and tripped forward onto the ground. Before I could pull myself up, Odin hopped on top of me, pushing his entire body-weight onto my chest, making it difficult to breathe. I reached out my arms and kicked out, trying to get him off of me. What the hell was happening? What was this guy's problem? He was crushing me and I gasped to try to catch my breath.

"Stop that, Odin!" a voice called out and I immediately recognized it to be Chelsea. I was surprised and I tried to lift my head so I could see her.

"What's that?" Odin said from on top of me, looking up at Chelsea, whose face was to the left of us.

Ames intervened, "Cool it every—"

"You heard me, Odin. Stop being such an ass!" Chelsea interrupted Ames, snapping at Odin in front of the silent crowd. I sensed an excited tension as everyone waited quietly to see what would happen next.

Odin laughed. "That . . . that is funny, Chelsea, coming from you," Odin yelled back as he continued to push me down with his forearm against my throat. I felt like I was choking, but I couldn't wiggle out from under Odin's weight.

"Okay, Odin," Ames said. He was standing right next to us. "I think you've made your point. Get off of him and help him up," he ordered, starting to pull Odin away from me. Odin sighed and then shifted his body weight. He grabbed my left forearm and lifted me up.

He stepped in toward me and poked his finger into the center of my chest forcefully. "Don't get in my way. I'm two fights away from getting out of here," he said. I didn't know how I was possibly involved in this.

"What are you talking about?" I asked.

"I've been hearing about you," he continued, glaring at me.

"Okay?" I was surprised he knew about me when I knew absolutely nothing about him or any of these other kids. He'd obviously been on the island for a while if he had eight wins—two away from getting out of here.

That rule seemed fishy to me. In my mind, it was highly unlikely that Gareth would let anybody leave the island that wasn't in Praeclarus, even if they earned it fair and square. That seemed way too risky.

As we stood there, I heard Delphine approaching.

"Boys, boys, okay boys, time to break it up—"

She snaked between us and looked up at Odin with that cute smile and he stepped back, the anger on his face dissipating ever so slightly. He then turned away to get a drink from the fountain.

Delphine moved in and pulled me in for a long, hard hug. I held her tight, not wanting to let go. I was just so happy she was alive. I looked over and saw Chelsea watching us, her arms folded across her chest.

"Reed. I thought you died. I'm thrilled to see you," Delphine said as she reached up and grabbed my face with both hands, like she was checking to make sure I was actually real.

"Me too. Do you know what happened to Micah? And what about everybody else?" I asked. I had so much I wanted to talk to her about, but it was obvious with everyone else looming around, we couldn't speak openly here.

"Hey, get outta here," Odin said to Delphine, as he walked back up to us. "I gotta show your pretty boy how to fight for real," he said.

He was probably just a few inches taller than me, but he was a physical beast—all muscle and coiled tension, like he could snap my neck at any moment.

I glanced up at the stands and saw Chelsea watching us closely. She didn't seem to notice anyone else and smiled down at me. Odin caught me looking at her and turned his attention toward me.

"You know Chelsea, huh?" he asked, but it was more like a demand than a question.

"Yeah, we know each other." I snapped back at him.

"Dip into that well at your own risk," he said, smirking.

Ames now stood next to us, listening in. "What's going on over here?" he asked. "Why aren't you training?"

"Leave them be, Ames!" Chelsea called out. "Odin always gives the guys he's most scared of the hardest time," she said.

"If you say so, Chelsea," Ames responded. "You boys can figure out whose balls are bigger. Just don't kill each other before you get to the Round again, okay?"

I nodded, glaring back at Odin. He looked like he wanted to strangle me right there.

We trained very hard for the rest of the day.

Ames ordered more challenging advanced grappling, karate, and weaponry exercises.

Throughout the day, I kept making eye contact with Delphine, but we never got the chance to talk one-on-one.

Odin stayed close to my side through every exercise, talking shit and trying to get a rise out of me, which caused everyone else besides Delphine great amusement. The boys in the group taunted me, rallying behind Odin, who everyone seemed to look up to as a leader. Chelsea watched everything and occasionally chided Odin in return for his bullying me, which only angered him more.

At the end of the day, I was exhausted. My shoulder hurt and I was covered in dirt, sweat, and blood from hours of brutal and exhausting exercises.

"Time to go eat and get some rest," Ames said, holding me back as the group filed out the door on the other side of the training yard. Delphine also hung back to try to talk to me, but the White Suits pushed her ahead.

"You okay?" Ames asked, looking me over.

"Yeah, I'm fine," I said, even though I couldn't help but feel annoyed. I wanted to strangle Odin the first chance I got. "What was that about?"

"You're a newbie. Don't worry about it," Ames said. "You gotta shake it off."

"What's up with Odin and Chelsea? Do they have a thing?" I asked.

Ames shrugged dismissively, "No, it's not that."

But, by the look on his face, I think he knew more than he was letting on.

"So . . . what's his problem with me?"

"I don't know, Reed, but you can't let Odin get under your skin."

I attempted to shrug him off, unsuccessfully. I was trying really hard to not let Odin's harassment get to me.

"Reed, I placed you with Odin so you can learn from him. He's that good—the best fighter the island has ever seen. That's why you gotta train with him, watch him closely, and learn as much as you can about him and how he fights. When you *do* match up—which I think will happen—you'll be ready," he said. "There's not much more I can do to help you."

"How are we going to reach out to my dad?" I asked.

He leaned in to talk to me quietly, looking back at the White Suit who was waiting at the door for us. "We're working on the plan as we speak. It involves re-tooling the computer systems on the island, which takes time. We just need to keep you alive, okay?"

I nodded, but the solution wasn't progressing fast enough. I didn't want to face the Coliseum again.

"What can I do to help now?"

"Not get killed," he said, nodding toward the Suit, who was out of earshot, but still waiting. "Let's go eat dinner, okay?"

I resigned myself to not getting any more answers tonight and begrudgingly followed him down the hallway to a large room, which had one long wooden table in its center. Everyone was already seated and I noticed the spot next to Delphine was open. I rushed over to sit next to her as she shoveled mashed potatoes into her mouth.

She looked over at me with an expression of relief.

"You're okay," she said, looking me up and down.

"You're okay," I responded, happy to see how healthy she appeared. A White Suit came and put down a plate of hot food in front of me. As much as I needed to talk to Delphine, more than anything I wanted to eat, and scarfed everything down quickly.

When I finally felt satisfied, I looked over at Delphine and she was smirking at me. "Hungry, huh?" she asked.

"You should talk," I joked, pointing to the

mashed potato glob on her chin. "Where is every-one else—from the boat?" I asked.

"Rose is gone," she blurted out, not realizing that I knew already.

"I know," I responded, reaching under the table to hold her hand and squeezing it hard. She squeezed it back.

"Carl's dead too, isn't he?" she asked, looking up at me, scared.

I nodded.

"I don't want to talk about it."

"Awww . . . are you guys comparing notes on your first kills?" Odin leaned across the table, eavesdropping. "That's so . . . cute," he said, and the boys sitting on his left and right—Mato and Ivan—laughed heartily.

Ivan was dark and pimply, and from earlier in the day, I knew he didn't speak English, but he seemed to understand it—or understand the nuances of what was happening. The other kid, Mato, spoke English, but was quiet. Whenever I caught eyes with him, he'd glare at me and then look away.

I wondered who these kids were and where they were from. There was no way Gareth was hijacking boats or groups of kids right and left without drawing attention to the disappearances, so I guessed they had to be taken in some other way.

"Shut up, Odin," Delphine barked across the table dismissively. He laughed in response and wiped his mouth clean with the back of his hand.

"I'd like nothing more than for you to come over here and make me," Odin said, standing up and gesturing at his crotch, getting the desired effect of a laugh out of Mato, Ivan, and the other boys sitting around them.

"Yeah right, you wish," Delphine snapped back and did that fake barfing thing she used to do when Sully hit on her.

Dessert was brought out and Odin turned his attention to his slice of pie. His friends followed suit, and I leaned in to Delphine.

"Where's Micah?" I asked.

"I have no idea. I heard Benny and Marcus were made into Suits, but I haven't seen Micah or heard anything about him since I was sent to the Coliseum," she said, taking a bite of pie.

As she ate, she looked at me seriously. "I know they've had more fights. I can hear them, but no one else from the boat has made it to this group. I don't know why we're so lucky," she said sarcastically.

"Yeah, we're blessed, huh?" I joked back, relieved to have someone to wallow in gallows humor with me.

"So, is it true about Chelsea?" she asked.

"What do you mean?"

"I'm not stupid, Reed. I can tell something is going on between you two, but I don't know what . . . or how . . . "

"Nothing is going on. She's become a friend, that's all," I said, realizing I probably sounded a little too defensive. I also didn't want Odin to hear the conversation, since there was obviously something weird happening between him and Chelsea.

"Do you think she can help get us out of here?" she asked. "You should try to get as much info as you can out of her. She must know a way off the island, right?" Delphine asked, looking at me hopefully.

"Maybe? She says she can help us escape, but I also wonder if she's just messing with me." I turned my attention to a big bite of my pie.

"She said that? That's interesting. Do you believe her?"

"I think so . . . "

"Well, you should totally hit and quit that," Delphine said, laughing at her own joke. "Just get her to tell you everything about her plan, and we'll figure out a way out of here together, okay?"

"Sure," I said, but I felt uneasy.

CHAPTER 7

My first night in the new training area I was taken to different living quarters. The rooms encircled a center communal space, like our first cells, but I didn't have to share my room with anyone else.

For the first week in this area, everyone yelled at each other through their bars and ignored me, except to taunt me and call me names. Delphine and I had little opportunity to talk, and the only time we got to have even semi-private conversations was when we were out in the training area and at meal times. Chelsea watched over our workout sessions nearly every day, but I hadn't been alone with her since the night she took me out to the mountain and game area.

She flirted with me in front of everyone, much to the anger of Odin. Then one day, Chelsea arrived on the floor while I was grappling with Mato.

We both stopped mid-wrestle as she walked in, draped in purple cloth that fell off her shoulders. She came over and sat cross-legged next to where Mato and I were fighting.

"Don't let me stop you," she said, and leaned over onto her elbows, so we could both clearly see down the top of her dress.

I glanced over and saw Odin standing just yards away with a wooden spear in hand. His face was turning red and when we caught eyes, he threw down his spear and stormed to the fountain for water. Chelsea laughed loudly, and everyone else was quiet.

Later, when I went to take a water break,

Chelsea came over to stand next to me. She rested against the wall and sighed.

"You look really good out there, Reed," she said, leaning into me. I felt everybody's eyes on the two of us.

"I think you're on the way to becoming the best fighter the island has ever seen," she continued, speaking loudly enough for the group to hear. "You're a natural."

Even though I sensed this was for show—to piss off Odin, as he stood just ten yards away with Ivan—I couldn't help but feel flattered that she chose to direct her advances toward me.

After she left that day, Delphine came over to me while I was standing on the sidelines, watching Mato and another kid, who everyone called "Teeth," punch each other.

"I'm guessing Odin and Chelsea have a thing, right?" she asked.

"I don't know for sure, but something is

weird with them. I think that's why he has it out for me."

"He's an asshole," Delphine said. "You should totally flirt with Chelsea just to fuck with him. Turn the screw a bit, right? He deserves it."

I smiled at her. "Yeah, I agree. Fuck Odin."

But in my gut, I wondered if there was more to the story. Why was Chelsea heaping praise on me? I was nowhere near as talented of a fighter as Odin. Was she doing this just to anger Odin? Flirting with her to piss him off didn't sound so bad.

As I was walking back to the living quarters for the night, Odin approached me on the left side and shoved me hard, causing me to stumble forward. I hit the dirt forcefully, my bad shoulder twinging in pain and my face scraping open. I felt blood on my chin and I heard people laughing over me—it was Odin and his asshole friends.

Before I could fully stand up, Delphine stormed over, yelling at Odin and the others.

"What the hell was that? Get back before I hurt

you myself," she spat in Odin's direction and they laughed at her.

"Oohh . . . I'm so terrified. Watch out for Delphine! She's such a badass!"

Delphine stomped over to me and helped to lift me up off of the ground.

I brushed the dirt off of myself and glared back at Odin. "Dude—you better watch yourself."

"What are you going to do . . . kill me?" he asked, laughing.

As Ames ushered us into our rooms that night, I caught eyes with Delphine and she gave me a look like she was worried about me.

I went to bed fuming, and plotted countless ways to get back at Odin to humiliate him. The worst thing would be to get Chelsea to kiss me in front of him. I fantasized about this scenario again and again. How could I make that happen?

More than anything, I wanted to hear the door code beep, for Chelsea to come into the room to be with me, to take me out of here, to take me to the top of the mountain and to plot a way to escape together. But she didn't come and whenever I heard footsteps outside the door, I excitedly glanced to see who it was. To my disappointment, it was always a White Suit making the rounds.

After a couple of weeks in the new training area, Ames told us that the next fights would be starting in two days. The announcement changed the energy in the space—the testosterone and adrenaline and fear in the air were palpable.

The rumor was that the Praeclarus Club members had arrived the previous day and were ready to see a fight.

We didn't know who would be chosen—there was no rhyme or reason that was explained to us. I just knew Ames took notes about our training, which he shared with Gareth.

As we warmed up the next morning, suddenly the door swung open and Gareth and Chelsea walked in. She had her arm linked in his. His hair gleamed silver and black under the sun and he smiled at us like he was some kind, grandfatherly figure, not the man who would take pleasure in seeing a handful of us die—or, perhaps, the man who enjoyed seeing his friends take pleasure in seeing a handful of us die. I wasn't sure what his motivations were exactly.

Chelsea and Gareth sat on the sidelines and watched us as we went through several training exercises.

Odin was next to me and I could tell he was trying to show off—it was obnoxious. He swung his sword around with such speed and vigor that I couldn't help but sneak glances at him.

Gareth appeared disinterested in Odin's showboating, and Ames stopped Odin short so Gareth could then watch others without interruption.

"Everyone else stop," Gareth said. "I want to see what Ivan can do—or can't do."

We all halted movement and Ivan stepped forward. He looked nervous, but he swung his sword around several times quickly. His movements were choppy and he didn't look very impressive at all. Even I could see that.

"I've witnessed enough!" Gareth yelled to Ivan. "Come up here right now, boy, so I can see you closer. I want to tell you something."

I glanced over at Ames who was frowning but unable to do anything. Ivan walked to the steps that led to where Gareth and Chelsea were sitting. Ivan's face was red, and I saw sweat dripping down his back. He stood in front of Gareth, who gestured at Ivan to come closer. Ivan leaned his head down and Gareth whispered something in his ear that we couldn't hear. Then, without any hesitation, Gareth suddenly snatched Ivan close to him and slit his neck with a sharp knife. Blood shot out and Ivan collapsed in front of Gareth. As quickly as it happened, two Suits ran up and dragged Ivan's body away. Gareth dabbed at the blood that covered his hands with a look of disgust, then turned to look at us.

We all stood silently. I couldn't believe what

I'd just witnessed. Why had he killed Ivan without warning?

"Sorry friends, but after so many days of trying to get Ivan to rise to the occasion, he just wasn't cutting it. He was grossly subpar," he said slowly, drawing out each word like it was its own sentence. No one spoke, not even Ames. Chelsea sat with a blank stare next to him, not betraying what I imagined she was really thinking.

"Okay, okay . . . enough of that business. I want to see you all and what you can do. Reed, let's see what you've got."

I stepped forward and I tried my best to look good, but as I swung my arm around, I could feel it shaking.

Gareth called me out almost immediately.

"Come on now, Reed. I know you're better than that. Are you trying to get yourself killed?"

"No, sir," I responded. I kept thrusting my sword, but felt my face turning hot with nervousness. I saw Odin laughing at me.

"That's enough, Reed," Gareth said. "I'm giving you the benefit of the doubt, for now."

I sat down with a cup of water, sweaty and tired, taking in the scene—there were nearly thirty kids in this current group. Since arriving at this training area, I learned that most kids had been stolen from various places from around the world, one by one. Their pictures were probably still displayed on frayed "MISSING" posters in their hometowns. Because they came from so many different places, I imagine that no one ever suspected they were all taken to the same place. Most were likely written off as runaways, or druggies who got mixed up in the wrong business, or sad kids trying to escape their shitty families.

Odin was different, though. I heard he had been on the island for longer than anyone else aside from Chelsea. The rumor was that he was the son of a staffer, and that he didn't have to fight until he did something that pissed off Gareth years ago. But this was just hearsay, so maybe none of that was true at all. My suspicions were that it had to do with Chelsea, but either no one I talked to knew the true story or they didn't want to share anything with me.

I looked over at Chelsea during the training session that morning and she refused to meet my gaze. Whenever her father was around, it was like I didn't exist.

I noticed Gareth watching someone closely and smiling, and I looked over to see who he was observing. My heart sank when I realized it was Delphine—he was eyeing her carefully, and I guessed by the way he was gazing at her with that smirk on his face, she was probably next to fight. I remembered him telling the crowd that he'd personally take care of her, and how much the crowd had loved her spitfire performance.

I wondered what sorts of things we'd face in the Coliseum now—at the Main Event—and if I'd escape fighting in the next round. If I could just lay low and not be chosen, that would give me time to try to track down Elise, to figure out the Titus connection, and for my parents to hopefully put together all of the pieces to find me before I had to kill again, or be killed.

We had a grand feast together for dinner that night, in the game room where we saw all the members' kills on display—tigers, an elephant, boars, exotic big cats, rhinos, and even animals I didn't recognize. They were marked with little gold plaques with names of who had killed them—some of the names I recognized, and others I couldn't place. There were a few movie stars, a couple of politicians, a basketball player, and a soccer star. I tried to memorize the names so I could expose all these terrible people if I ever escaped.

I realized some of these people were probably business associates of my dad's, and I wondered how many knew me. I also wondered if it was public knowledge in the real world that I had disappeared at sea. I couldn't help but think I had been targeted specifically because of my dad.

That night, all of these questions rolled around

in my head like loose marbles, and I couldn't sleep. Even though I wasn't ready to fight again, I questioned if there was any truth to the "ten win" rule. It didn't make sense. I thought back to what Odin told me earlier, taunting me—

"I'm getting out of here . . . only a few wins away and I'll be free. Gareth's going to put me on a boat to freedom, with millions in the bank. An offshore bank account—"

"Why would Gareth do that?" I asked, pushing back. It sounded like bullshit. No way Gareth would risk his secrets being exposed to let one of us go. It was way too dangerous. So that meant that he was either lying about that rule or he knew that no one would ever reach ten wins.

Odin scowled at me.

"Gareth is all about making his own laws—and the ten-win rule is one of the island's most important ones. He talks about it at the beginning of fights—everyone knows that's the way it is."

"But no one has ever reached ten fights, right?"

Odin scoffed. "Not yet, but that's because there's never been a fighter like me . . . "

I rolled around under my sheets and felt restless.

I heard the kids in adjacent rooms get quieter and quieter, until eventually, I sensed from the stillness of the room that I was the only one still awake.

I wondered if I'd see Micah and the others tomorrow. Where were they?

I was listening to everyone's snores when suddenly I heard slow, quiet footsteps approaching. I looked up and saw Elise enter my room. Her long, dark hair framed her face wildly, and her eyes were wide.

It was the first time I'd seen her since after I'd been injured in my first fight, when she cared for my wounds. I had the sense then that there was more that she wanted to tell me, and that she was the type of person that loved to talk—to anyone and everyone.

"I'm not supposed to be here," she said, whispering urgently. "I'm not going to be able to help you yet, so you gotta survive, okay?" she said. "And take this," she said, shoving something cold and small into my hand.

I looked down. She had given me a gold locket with an ornate design carved into it. When I opened it, I saw a photo of a young Elise with a baby.

"I wear it always, but now I think you're the one who needs the luck," she said.

"Who is this?" I asked, but in the distance, we heard two White Suits talking to each other in muffled voices, starting to approach. Elise got up and ran off, silently sliding the door closed that led to the hallway.

CHAPTER 8

I couldn't sleep the rest of the night—I thought about Carl dying underneath me with that look of disbelief on his face. I wondered what would happen in the morning.

When the sun began to rise, Ames came to retrieve us with several White Suits in tow.

"Well, come on now, you're all heading to the big show," he said matter-of-factly. The Suits methodically went door-to-door, opening each one and letting us all out.

Before I left my room, I stuffed Elise's locket under my mattress because there was nowhere else to put it. Where could I possibly hide it if I was made to change clothing to fight?

We were ushered to a holding cell next to the Coliseum, where we dressed in the white warrior costumes and got painted, one by one. This was a different setup than last time and I didn't know what it all meant. We heard the crowd's cheers on the other side of the metal gate and Gareth's muffled voice, making announcements that must've excited the group, causing them to yell louder and louder.

Ames had us huddle around him, and Odin shoved past me to get to the front.

Ames kept glancing down at his wristlet any time it buzzed and the screen went bright. He looked down at it repeatedly as we waited. Finally, he got the answer he was waiting for.

"Mato. You're up."

"Who's he fighting?" Odin demanded, looking troubled.

"A newbie," Ames responded and everyone turned to look at me.

"No, not Reed. C'mon, let's go to the viewing

area. Mato, you stay behind. And good luck to you, my friend."

Mato's face was pale and he stared blankly down at his feet. We walked away from him, leaving him alone as the giant gate lifted and the White Suits prodded him to move forward into the arena.

Ames took us up a flight of stone stairs and as we reached the top, I was surprised to see that we were standing now on a platform enclosed by Plexiglas, looking down at the Coliseum arena floor.

I saw spectators scattered around the ring, and Gareth and Chelsea presiding over the activities from their box seats. Chelsea looked up in our direction and I thought she was looking right at me, but I couldn't be sure.

She smiled wide before turning around to face the ring again, and now I stared at the back of her head. Just past her, down on the arena floor, I saw Mato, and even from my vantage point so high up,

I could tell he was shaking. He had not been given a weapon yet, and I wondered who he'd face.

Just then, the gate on the other side of the Coliseum opened and someone walked through, followed by three White Suits. From this view, even so far away, I knew it was Micah.

I couldn't help myself, and I screamed out at him. "Micah! Micah! You have to kill him!"

He didn't look my way. Ames snapped at me, "Shut up, Reed!"

"Micah! He's going to kill you!"

I realized he couldn't hear me over the other people screaming at him. He was too far away. He looked around bewildered, but he didn't glance up in our direction. I saw Gareth turn back to us briefly and motion to a Suit standing guard next to him.

I reached down to take off my shoe and was about to chuck it over the plexi wall to try to get Micah's attention, but as I stooped over, a White Suit zapped me and I screamed out in pain.

It was the same searing burn from when Titus attacked me on the boat. I spun around and the Suit was looming over me, with Ames by his side.

"You've gotta control yourself, Reed," Ames warned, looking at me like he was disappointed. I guessed the subtext was about our previous conversations, even if he couldn't say it directly.

I was still hunched over when Delphine came over to help lift me up. We watched helplessly as Mato and Micah prepared to face off.

"Why are we here?" Delphine wondered aloud, exasperated. "This is sadistic, you know," she said to Ames, who pulled out his tablet to take notes.

"Why? To psyche you out if you're next," Odin chimed in, and I realized he was standing right behind us now. He looked bored, and pointed down to the Coliseum floor.

"Is that your buddy? A kid from the boat?" Odin asked, nodding downward. I didn't answer. "It's a shame he's got to go this way," he said. "Mato is going to carve him up."

Before I knew it, Gareth was speaking, telling the crowd about the amazing fight they were about to witness, playing up the strengths of Mato and the newcomer Micah. Everyone howled in excitement as the match started and the crowd cried out again and again, as Micah and Mato circled each other, given no weapons but their hands. Neither one would strike first and I felt the men in the crowd start to turn on them, everyone growing restless and tired of waiting for bloodshed.

Delphine gripped my arm and all of a sudden the gates lifted again and White Suits came out carrying metal canisters in their hands.

"What are they doing?" Delphine asked and I shrugged. Before Mato or Micah could react, the Suits poured gasoline in a circle around where Mato stood. Mato looked terrified as a White Suit lit a match and threw it his way, causing him to be encircled by a sudden rush of flames. He screamed out, which I both saw and heard in high definition on the Coliseum's jumbo screen.

Mato suddenly rushed forward through the flames and tackled Micah to the ground. Micah grunted in surprise and threw Mato off of his chest. He scanned his surroundings and grabbed a rock that was a few feet away, throwing it hard at Mato's face, and striking him in the forehead, causing it to split open. Blood rushed down Mato's face, appearing to blind him momentarily. Micah stormed forward, taking advantage of Mato's temporary weakness and brought him down to the ground in one swift, powerful motion. They both fell to the dirt and rolled around violently, poking and gouging and kicking and punching at each other.

Blood poured into Mato's eyes and he reached his arms up to try to stop his opponent. Micah now put his hands around Mato's neck and gripped hard, Mato's body struggling and bucking under his weight for about a minute until it was suddenly totally still.

The men and women in the crowd applauded

and Micah let go of Mato, whose body collapsed in unnatural angles beneath him.

I was surprised to see Micah beat Mato so easily—it seemed like he wasn't strained at all. As Micah was ushered away, he glanced around, appearing to fully take in his surroundings, and then he looked up toward the sky. I saw him spot me and Delphine as we waved our arms down at him. Surprised, he called out our names. But as the crowd's yells grew louder again and music blared through the amphitheater, we couldn't hear anything at all over the noise.

As we stood there, Ames came up to me and looked at me with a serious nod toward the floor. "You're next, my friend."

"What? Why me? I'm not doing this again!" I spat at him, pushing him away from me.

"Gareth's orders, I'm afraid. Now don't make this more difficult."

"Who am I up against?"

"I don't know, Reed. This request just came

in," he said, pushing me toward the White Suit, who yanked my arm and pulled me out the door. Delphine grabbed the other arm and tried to keep me inside.

I screamed out and tried to dig in my heels. I grabbed at the railing and reached back toward Delphine, howling as I was being dragged away. She looked at me with wide eyes and called out for me, but there was nothing either of us could do.

I didn't want to die.

We both knew it was worthless, trying to stop the Suits from taking me, and they yanked me away from her and down the stairs that led to the rooms where fighters got ready.

As I got dressed into the warrior outfit, I heard the crowd chanting my name over the loudspeakers. I felt nauseated and I thought if I threw up right there, maybe I'd be given a reprieve. But, before I had the opportunity to consider this seriously, I was pulled through the hallway that led to the big metal gate that opened into the Coliseum.

The White Suits dragging me out refused to look at me, and I wondered if they'd been stolen away or come to the island of their own free will. Maybe if I just tried to reason with them, they'd let me go and I could make a run for it. But just then, the gate rose and they forcefully yanked me out onto the Coliseum floor.

When I got out to the center of the dirt area, I looked up at the crowd, and they all yelled down at me, throwing things in my direction. A half-eaten turkey leg bounced off my chest onto the ground, and I glared up at the direction from where it came.

As I stood there, waiting for my opponent to be brought out, I caught eyes with Chelsea, who quickly looked away.

"I think everyone will be surprised who Reed is up against today, perhaps Reed most of all," Gareth said. I wondered what he could mean, and I turned to face the gate. It slowly opened and an extremely tall, shirtless guy wearing a black hood over his head was ushered in by two White Suits. He was squirming and fighting against them with all of his might.

I didn't recognize the person, and I went through everyone I knew in my brain and all the kids from the training area, trying to figure out who it could possibly be.

I glanced up and saw Delphine, her arms pressed up against the clear plastic panels, like she was trying to break through. She was yelling something and pointing toward Gareth, but I couldn't hear her over the crowd's cheers.

As I looked at the spectators, I saw a familiar face sitting next to Gareth. Titus. It *was* him. I was one hundred percent sure now. But how was he involved, exactly?

I didn't have time to think about it more than an instant, or to react to seeing Titus sneering down at me, as Gareth spoke once again—"This is a person that's tormented Reed, that's caused him great physical pain. Reed—would you like to take one free shot at him?"

Gareth looked down at me bemused, but I didn't respond at first, trying to guess his angle. Was he tricking me?

"Reed . . . take the weapon," Gareth instructed and one of the White Suits handed me a blunt wooden club, with spikes encircling its tip.

"One strike likely won't kill him outright, but it will give you an advantage in your fight. Don't you want that Reed? Isn't that the smart thing to do?"

I didn't know who the hooded person was, and I thought this could very well be some sort of game that Gareth was playing. I didn't want to hurt a masked, defenseless person. What if it was actually someone I knew and loved? But who could it be? The man was struggling violently against the grip of the Suits holding him in place.

"No," I yelled out. "I don't want that," I said. The crowd booed at me loudly.

"Are you sure, Reed? This may be a life or

death decision," Gareth warned but I couldn't bring myself to hurt someone unprovoked and unable to defend himself.

"I'm sure."

"Suit yourself, Reed. Take off his hood please, gentlemen, and give the club to our friend there instead," Gareth said, gesturing toward the masked person. The White Suit next to me walked over with the weapon in hand. They removed the hood slowly and I couldn't help but gasp in surprise. It was True, from Ship Out, the asshole that tortured me day after day on the boat and subjected me to physical and mental humiliation, weeks at a time. My tormentor. He was alive, but why was he here—and as a fighter?

He turned right and left with quickness, glancing around with a look of panic on his face. I got the sense he was seeing everything in the Coliseum for the first time.

"Your job is to kill each other, or be killed. It's that simple," Gareth instructed and the White

Suit next to True handed him the club. True, as if understanding the two possibilities for how this could end, grabbed the weapon and stormed toward me immediately.

Before I could think twice, my training instantly kicked in and I dodged out of the way at the last moment as True ran in my direction. True stopped in his tracks and circled back at me. As he was about to charge with his arm raised, he stopped suddenly, his face contorting in anger as he looked up in the crowd.

"You!" he screamed up in Gareth's direction, and I turned and saw who he was screaming at. It wasn't Gareth—it was Titus. I could tell because Titus waved down at us with a smile.

"You lied to me!" True screamed at Titus, who was looking down at him. "I'm going to kill you!" he yelled, and I recognized his distracted fury toward Titus as an invaluable moment of weakness. I had to take action now.

Without thinking any more about it, I snatched

the zapping instrument out of the hand of the White Suit standing next to me and charged at True, reaching out my arm and buzzing him forcefully with a jolt of electricity until he collapsed to the ground, screaming in pain.

He fell into a large lump and dropped the club at his side. I grabbed it off the ground, and as the crowd shrieked, I hit True hard across the head, causing blood to shoot out and splash me. I smashed his head over and over and over again, exhausting myself with each swing, as blood splattered on my face. Everyone went crazy—the screams suddenly jarring me out of a trance—and I snapped out of it. True's head was caved in. I dropped the club and looked at my surroundings, bewildered. That had come *too* easy; it frightened me.

What did I just do? And without even a second thought? I looked up in Delphine's direction, and she had turned away. Then I glanced at Chelsea, and she was smiling, whispering something to her dad.

True was moaning, incapacitated, and I staggered away from him. No one came to assist him and he sat there heaving in pain. Then, moments later, True began to plead for help, his voice twisting in anguish. Soon, his cries became gurgled and it sounded like he was choking on his own blood. As I stood there awkwardly considering what to do to next, True was already dead. It was obvious.

I was taken back to a special room after the battle to shower, and as I stood with the hot water running over my back, the same questions entered my head again and again: Why was True thrown into the Coliseum to fight me? And what had happened between him and Titus? Was True involved in Praeclarus at all? I had no answers, but felt even more unsettled. I was nearly certain now that our arrival here was no coincidence.

When I got back to the living quarters that

night, everyone else was waiting at their doors and clapped loudly when I came in. I was surprised by the warm welcome.

"Dude, that was incredible," one kid said to me. "You caught him off-guard and bam! You're so lucky, man!"

"Yeah, luck is the right word," Odin yelled out at me sarcastically. I ignored him as I retreated into my room. I just wanted to sleep and forget all about this place for a few hours.

Utterly exhausted, I passed out within minutes, and slept like a rock for the first time in days.

Over the next three weeks, I fought twice more, each time against boys in the elite camp that were friends of Odin. One was a kid named Elias, who I stabbed in the back repeatedly after he hit me in the head with a club in a glancing blow, knocking me sideways but not off my feet. A new ferocious coolness was emerging from within me, and with each stab, the crowd cheered, calling out my name again and again like I was a rock star or a pro athlete. And because I was becoming a stronger fighter, a tiny part of me felt satisfied, which scared me.

The other kid I took out was this asshole named Joss who liked to taunt me alongside Odin during training and made it his goal to push me whenever my back was turned. During our battle, we wrestled, gouging at each other's eyes. He tried to kick me hard in the balls, but missed by just a bit. I pretended to be doubled over in pain, and when he came over to deal me the final blow, I jumped forward and tackled him to the ground and punched his face repeatedly before I used my thumbs to gouge out his eyes and then strangle him.

I didn't know what had come over me. It was like a mean, vengeful person was tearing its way out of me, clawing to get out, and the Praeclarus crowd loved this new, aggressive Reed. They made me feel like I was special, and better at the fights in the Round than anyone else—except for Odin.

One day, I got to watch Odin fight in the Coliseum for the first time. He was quick and ruthless and was about to take his opponent out within seconds, like it was no big deal, when the crowd jeered and he stopped, holding the poor kid underneath him with his knife raised. Praeclarus loved him—but they wanted a more interesting fight, which Gareth reminded him by yelling down to make it a better match. So, instead of killing the kid immediately, Odin let him scramble away for a moment before charging at him and tackling him to the ground easily, laughing. He did this a few times, like he was a cat, toying with a gravely injured rodent. But the crowd loved this game, and they cheered his theatrics enthusiastically. Even I had to admit he was extremely impressive, with the way in which he conquered and utterly owned his opponent, a kid who had looked tough throughout training.

When he won, I noticed him look at Gareth and Chelsea, Chelsea's mouth wide open, laughing, and clapping her hands together over and over and over again.

CHAPTER 9

After he had recovered from his first battle, Micah was moved to our training area. When he came through the door, I ran over to him and we hugged. Delphine stopped what she was doing and joined us. Micah picked her up and swung her around, making Delphine squeal, but I caught him wincing.

"I'm so glad you're both here," Micah said. "What is this place?" he asked and I looked around to see who was listening. Everyone else was gathered around the new chest of swords Ames and Max had brought out.

"Let's talk at dinner," I said, looking back at the group. No one seemed to be listening to us.

"But, I'm working on a way to get us out of here," I said, and Delphine raised her eyebrows.

"How?" Micah asked, leaning in to hear me. Just then, Ames yelled out for us to come over to begin the morning's training.

"Let's talk tonight," I said. As we walked over to join the group, Micah reached over and punched me on the arm and gave me a smile. Even in these circumstances, he conveyed a confidence and made me feel like everything was going to be okay, somehow. I hoped Micah and I would never have to fight.

Later that day during training, Ames came over to me and pulled me aside. "You've made quite the impression, Reed. You're many people's favorite fighter now. They're starting to put big money on your matches," he continued. I knew I should feel worried, but secretly, I enjoyed the adulation, the cheers of the crowd, and the perks that came along with winning. I got special dinners after each fight, massages, free time in the

training yard, and pretty much anything else I asked for—except freedom.

I wanted to get Ames alone to hear updates on the escape plan, but I couldn't figure out a way to talk to him without alerting suspicions. And, I couldn't help but wonder if Ames was being totally honest with me. To make matters worse, Elise was never by herself when I saw her. I passed her in the hallways and she always gave me a look like *don't you dare say anything*. I didn't want to blow either of our covers. I'd have to wait until someone came to talk to me, which was becoming torturous as I worried about being put into the Coliseum again. It was only a matter of time until my luck ran out.

It had also been a while since I'd gotten to be with Chelsea alone. She didn't come to visit me, and during training sessions, she'd barely glance in my direction. She seemed distracted and unhappy, and when Ames tried to joke around with her, she looked disinterested. I wondered if I did something to make her angry.

I caught Odin trying to get her attention sometimes, but she wouldn't give him the time of day either.

Odin was supposedly one victory away from freedom, so he walked around like an even bigger asshole, with his chest puffed out, smug and insufferable. He talked shit to everyone about how he was leaving this place once and for all. I'd be more annoyed by his bullshit if I didn't feel slightly bad for him—if he *really* thought he was getting out of here, he was dumber than I initially thought.

Then, in the middle of the night one evening, while I was sleeping deep and dreamless, I felt something hit my bed, waking me up.

I jolted upwards and something small flung off of me, bouncing with a quiet ping across the floor. I looked out at the door. In the darkness, I barely made out Chelsea standing there. She glanced around, making sure no one else had woken up. It was very risky for her to be here, where she could definitely be found out if anyone stirred or heard us talking.

The door quietly beeped and she slid in. To my surprise, she was wearing just a small, white nightgown. She was barefoot and her hair fell over her shoulders.

"I'm sorry I haven't seen you in a while. I haven't been able to. I'm in trouble," Chelsea whispered, reaching out and pulling me in to a hug. She grabbed me tightly.

"What are you talking about?" I asked, half asleep and very confused.

"Odin knows I'm trying to plan an escape with you." She glanced across the way to his cell, but everyone remained asleep.

"Wait . . . what do you mean? How does he know that?" I asked, whispering too as I knew it would be disastrous to be found out.

"I don't know, honestly. Anyway, he confronted

me about it and he told my dad that you and I are hooking up. And now my dad's going to have Odin murder you—just to spite me," she was talking quietly, but very quickly.

"What? Slow down. What do you mean?"

I couldn't see her very well in the darkness but I could tell she had been crying.

"Gareth was going to kill you outright. Do it in front of all the staff and me—to prove a point . . . that's what he does . . . but Odin said he wanted to fight you himself, that he'd take great pleasure in taking you out. You've really pissed him off. And, he's such a kiss-up to my dad, he'd do anything to try to impress him or gain his favor," Chelsea said. She began to cry again very quietly and I held her tight against me. "You're going to be facing Odin in the next battle, Reed—and it's just two days from now."

I let those words sink in. I didn't feel confident on my odds of getting out alive against Odin. He was that good.

"Calm down. It will be okay. I can handle it," I said, although I wasn't so sure, if I was being honest.

"I don't think so, Reed," Chelsea whispered, but then started sobbing, choking her cries into my blanket to stay quiet. "Unless . . . "

"Unless what?"

"I think I can help you beat Odin," she finally said. "I've watched every one of his fights. I've seen him in training every day. He is ruthless and he must be stopped. I can help you defeat him. You'll take him out, and we'll get out of here. I finally have an idea of how to do it. We don't need to wait for Ames and Elise. They're taking too long," she said, reaching over to get in my lap. She curled up in a ball on top of me, the bare skin of her thighs pressing against mine.

"What do you mean? How?" I asked. No one would tell me anything concrete to help us get out of here, and I was starting to feel very impatient.

"I know how to contact your dad," Chelsea said.

"What? How?"

"I can't explain it. You have to see what I'm talking about. I'll show you after your fight. I promise. There's no way I'll be able to take you there without them catching on before the fight. They're on to us."

"So, what should I do?"

"Odin's weakness—his Achilles heel—is me," she said. "We used to be lovers," she said, and even though it wasn't a surprise really, the news still stung. I was quiet. "Are you jealous?" Chelsea asked, reaching up to touch my face. I pulled away.

"No, I'm fine . . . so, how are we going to do this?"

"During the fight, I'll jump down to the floor and you'll need to pretend you're about to kill me. That will catch Odin off guard, and you'll be able to strike. You'll only have a moment, but that's all you'll need. You're the only one who can do this. It will be okay—I promise," she said. She was quiet, but sounded assured. "It's the only thing I can think of that will work. He's too strong otherwise. You need to surprise him. He'll do anything to protect me—which makes him vulnerable."

"I don't understand. Why do you want Odin dead?" I asked, feeling uncertain.

"It's too long of a story to recount in detail, but Odin tried to hurt me. He took advantage of me, actually—"

"What?" I asked. "What do you mean?"

"I can't say exactly, but he's not a good person and I need your help to stop him before he does more . . . " she said.

"Okay," I responded, not wanting to push too much about what he'd done since it was upsetting her. I thought everything over to try to uncover the weakness in the plan. "But what about your dad? Won't he hurt you if you act out and defend me?"

"My dad would never harm me. I'm the only thing he's ever loved," she said. She stared at me with those big, brown eyes and I was determined to do whatever was necessary to help her. She hugged me tightly and then was gone again.

I looked around and no one seemed to be awake. I breathed a sigh of relief and thought about the plan the rest of the night.

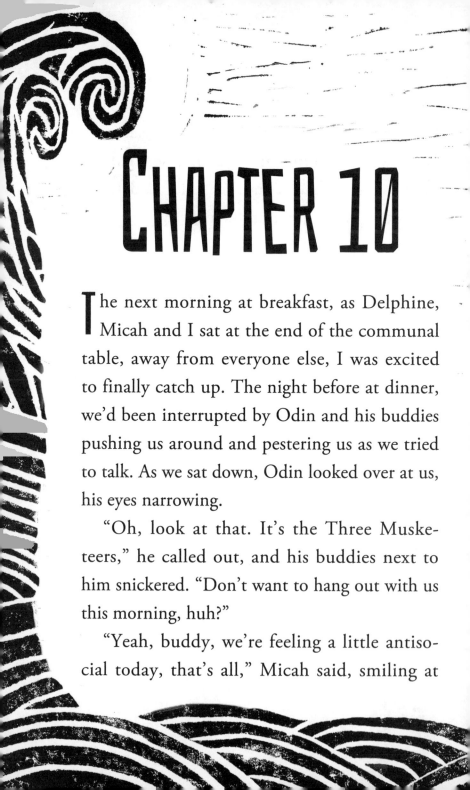

CHAPTER 10

The next morning at breakfast, as Delphine, Micah and I sat at the end of the communal table, away from everyone else, I was excited to finally catch up. The night before at dinner, we'd been interrupted by Odin and his buddies pushing us around and pestering us as we tried to talk. As we sat down, Odin looked over at us, his eyes narrowing.

"Oh, look at that. It's the Three Musketeers," he called out, and his buddies next to him snickered. "Don't want to hang out with us this morning, huh?"

"Yeah, buddy, we're feeling a little antisocial today, that's all," Micah said, smiling at

Odin. Odin relaxed a little and nodded his head like everything was cool. Micah had that way with people.

"Okay, man. Suit yourself," he said, turning to shovel the eggs and potatoes on his plate into his big mouth.

"What's going on?" Delphine asked.

"The bad news is that we have another battle scheduled tomorrow," I said, and Delphine and Micah both frowned, glancing at each other. "And, the even worse news is that I'm going to be up against Odin in the Round," I said.

"Are you sure?" Micah asked, looking concerned.

"How do you know that?" Delphine asked, looking to the side to make sure no one else was listening in.

"Chelsea told me," I said.

"When did she tell you this?" Micah asked.

"Last night. She came to see me in my cell in the middle of the night."

"I've heard that before—but this time I actually believe you. That's pretty ballsy," he said. "So, why would she tell you that? What else did she say?"

"She told me what I need to do to beat Odin," I explained.

"What did she tell you exactly, Reed? Do you trust her?" Delphine asked.

"Yes, I do. She wants off the island too, and she knows how to reach my dad, but I need to survive facing Odin."

"Do you think you can do it?" Delphine asked.

"Of course he can," Micah said, not letting me answer, and grabbing my shoulder and squeezing. "He's better than Odin, he just needs to prove it."

"Yeah, exactly," Delphine said, but she sounded uncertain. "Chelsea better help us out of here."

"She and I have a strategy, don't worry. She's going to distract Odin during the fight, and I'll take him down. She's his weakness, just watch."

"Sounds like you have it all figured out. Cheers to that, man," Micah said, raising his glass of orange juice. "But, you gotta go in believing you can win," he said, and I smiled back.

With a little bit of trickery, I felt like it was possible that I could take Odin out, but I didn't feel as assured as Micah. I picked up my cup and tapped his glass, feeling just a tiny bit optimistic for the first time in a long while.

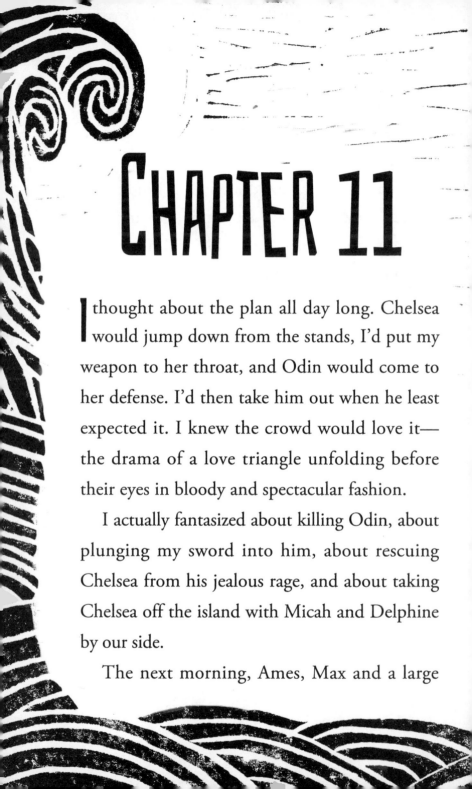

CHAPTER 11

I thought about the plan all day long. Chelsea would jump down from the stands, I'd put my weapon to her throat, and Odin would come to her defense. I'd then take him out when he least expected it. I knew the crowd would love it— the drama of a love triangle unfolding before their eyes in bloody and spectacular fashion.

I actually fantasized about killing Odin, about plunging my sword into him, about rescuing Chelsea from his jealous rage, and about taking Chelsea off the island with Micah and Delphine by our side.

The next morning, Ames, Max and a large

group of White Suits came to get all of us from our cells.

"Come on now. Gareth has requested the whole group," Ames said as they released all of us from our rooms. He led us down the hallway and we were all quiet. Usually everyone told jokes, but on the days of matches, the mood was always tense and silent. Especially today, when no one else knew who was fighting.

We went to the prep area and a team got us ready, giving us our outfits and painting us with vivid streaks of paint in many colors.

"Body paint—weird choice, huh?" Micah said, joking to me, as if he was trying to release the tension in the room, and within me. "The funny thing is, put this paint on me and I feel amazing," he said, checking himself out in the large mirrors that lined the room. Everyone laughed and I grinned back at him, but my heart was beating furiously in my chest. I hoped it wouldn't be the last time that I'd see my own reflection.

Once we were all ready, we stood there awkwardly, waiting for the news about who was up to fight. I tried to smile and look more confident than I felt. I glanced over at Odin, who loomed tall over the rest of us. He caught my eyes and gave me a dirty look. He'd get what was coming to him, I thought to myself, no longer minding his attempts to get under my skin.

I was expecting to be called at any moment, and Micah stood next to me. He put his hand on my shoulder and squeezed it tightly.

"You're going to do great, man. Keep the faith," he said. I wanted to believe him and stay positive, but I was feeling nervous.

Ames stood in front of us, looking down at his wristlet and waiting for the official word on who was fighting first. Suddenly, his device lit up and buzzed and he stared down at it with a surprised look on his face.

"Delphine—you're up," he said and I could sense a hint of regret in his voice. I was shocked.

Not Delphine. Anyone but Delphine. I thought it was my time. I'd much rather go in than see Delphine fight.

"Okay . . . who am I fighting?" she finally asked, looking resolved.

"It doesn't say, I'm afraid."

That didn't sound good and everyone was silent. The group had grown to like Delphine. It was impossible not to like her, really. She was cute, funny, sarcastic, a flirt, and made light of shitty situations, but the mood was heavy now as we left her to go upstairs to the viewing platform.

Micah and I hung back and Micah gave her a quick hug, his paint smudging her white clothing. As I pulled her in tight, I wondered if this was the last time I'd see her, but tried to smile to not show how nervous I was for her.

"We've got this," I said, as a White Suit grabbed me and pulled me toward the door. I looked up at the person.

"Trevor? Is that you?"

It *was* Trevor—from the Ship Out boat. I recognized his pimply face and shaggy hair peeking out under his hat. He broke a smile just for a split second when he saw that I spotted him.

"So you're a Suit?" I whispered as we went up the hallway. Micah turned around as well, glancing at us. "And Benny and Marcus?"

"Yeah. I guess we're too weak or ugly for the big game, so here I am," Trevor said, shrugging. "I don't know what's in store for me in the long run, but I'm glad to be a Suit versus, you know . . . " he stopped, realizing he might be making me feel like shit.

"Versus me? A fighter?"

He turned bright red. "I'm sorry man, I didn't mean it—"

"I know," I said. "It's okay. And besides, I'm going to figure out how to get us out of here."

He raised his eyebrows, but quickly said, "Shhh dude. I don't want to hear about it. You're going to get us both killed," as he nudged me up toward the stairs and wouldn't look at me in the eye again.

It seemed unfair. He got off easy—a lifetime as a Suit or a few weeks to months as a fighter. But truthfully, when pressed, I wasn't sure which option I'd choose.

He trailed us as we went up the tall staircase. I heard the group inside the Coliseum becoming rowdy, awaiting the day's first fight. I racked my brain trying to figure out who Delphine would be facing, if it wasn't any of us in the elite group.

We got up to the platform and looked down. It was a beautiful day; the sun shone bright and the air was warm. For an instant, it took me back to the day that James died. That was also a clear day, and the reason we headed out to the lake so early together that morning.

I wasn't ready to lose another person that I cared for and I hoped that Delphine would be able to fight off whoever she faced. I was determined to make sure she'd escape with us. We were all getting off this island together, one way or another.

The crowd started chanting her name "DEL-PHINE! DEL-PHINE! DEL-PHINE!" as she came through the gate. Her long red hair was tied in a thick braid that rested over her shoulder. She was tan from weeks of training in the sun. Every time there was a close-up of her face on the big screen—her eyes set with fierceness and determination—the crowd cheered. When she was in a warrior mode, that's when she looked the prettiest.

Suddenly, Gareth began talking. "It actually pains me, this match-up. You see, I've taken a liking to Delphine. She's quite feisty, which I enjoy immensely. But, that's why I think she'll be very entertaining in this battle. And, if she makes it out alive, I have even bigger plans for this little lady," Gareth said, looking down at her.

"Delphine. I hear you're an animal-lover. Is that true?"

Delphine just glared back at him and didn't say

anything in response. Micah and I stood watching, unable to help her from behind the wall.

"Well everyone, we're ready to finally debut a special feature. Something I've been toying with for quite some time, actually," Gareth said and the crowd quieted, waiting anxiously to see what new thing he'd be bringing to the fight. "And if you like *this*, I promise this is a precursor to something even more spectacular that will change everything you believe in your core about the limits of human achievement."

Everyone clapped and I wondered what the hell he could be talking about.

"Anyway, that is just a carrot. I can't share more yet, I'm afraid. But I am confident you'll enjoy what you see today. You all ready?" Gareth asked and the energy of the crowd grew more frenzied. I looked over at Micah, concerned.

"What can we do to help?" I asked, but Micah just shrugged back at me, as there was nothing we could do.

Delphine stood there, sword raised upwards, at the ready for whatever she faced. She didn't look as scared this time, but instead appeared determined.

"Okay, let's bring her in," Gareth ordered and the crowd turned their attention to the gate, which slowly rose. I saw something being wheeled in. It was a large, silver cage.

"What's in there?" I asked Micah, straining to see better.

As the Suits got closer, I saw there was a large, tan creature inside the cage, and that the animal was pacing back and forth quickly.

"Holy shit! That's a mountain lion!" Micah called out.

"Now *that's* crazy," Odin said, sounding genuinely scared. Everyone started to talk to each other excitedly, disbelieving what Delphine was about to face.

On the giant screen, I saw Delphine's eyes were

now wide with fear. None of us expected a wild animal as an opponent.

"You may recognize this beautiful creature. Or maybe she'll look more familiar when she's running, as most of you have only seen her in motion, when she's trying to hide from you," Gareth said. "Yes, this is our mountain lion from the game reserve."

The crowd cheered.

Gareth continued, "I thought it was time to see her fight, instead of hide. What do you all think?" The men and women sitting in the stands yelled out their approval.

The lion was very agitated. I heard it snarling in its cage, and it was pacing back and forth rapidly.

Delphine looked genuinely scared now. How does one fight a creature that doesn't react the same way as a human? Ames hadn't trained us for this.

I felt hopeless again and wished there was something—anything—I could do to help her. If there was a way to survive this, we'd stage a revolt. I was pretty sure we could get enough of the fighters and staff on our side to get out of here.

Chapter 12

As Delphine stood there, waiting, a Suit came to lift the gate latch of the lion's enclosure. As the cage opened and it was suddenly free, the lion sprinted out and charged at the Suit immediately, jumping up and grabbing onto the man's shoulders and taking him down, causing the crowd to shriek in excitement. The Suit screamed and punched, trying to kick the creature off of him, but the lion was holding on tight. The man cried out as the beast swiftly bit into his throat, tearing at it. The Suit went limp as the lion shook his body back and forth. Now that the Suit was unmoving, the creature lost interest, sniffed the body once more and then started to walk away.

She now looked up at Delphine, just thirty yards away.

To my surprise, Delphine began to move forward toward the creature. She raised her hands over her head, waving her sword in her right hand, with an upright, aggressive stance and as she walked toward the lion, she yelled at it loudly.

"I'm going to kill you! Get out of here! Aaaaghh! Aaagghh!"

The spectators thought this was hilarious, and started laughing, but the creature looked confused. The lion lowered her shoulders and her head and her ears went flat. You could tell that she was uneasy by this strange human approaching her aggressively.

She snarled and I saw on the screen that her collar had a mic on it—Gareth really thought of everything, didn't he?

I wondered how this standoff could possibly

end—there was nowhere for either opponent to escape to, and nowhere to hide.

Delphine continued yelling, puffing up her small body to look as big as possible. The lion slowly took one step backwards.

Suddenly, someone from the crowd screamed something indecipherable into a megaphone and then a large object went flying through the air and landed right behind the beast, startling her and causing her to jump forward toward Delphine, who now was just about ten yards away.

Delphine lunged out of the way and ran around the lion, which then spun around to charge at Delphine.

Delphine dropped her sword and swung down to pick up the large stone that had landed in the ring. As the lion ran right at her, Delphine flung the rock forward with all her might, hitting the animal squarely in the face and causing it to stumble backwards, stunned.

The lion snarled loudly and charged back at

Delphine who had quickly scooped up her sword to protect herself. The animal grabbed at Delphine's calf with its claws, taking her down to the ground hard.

Delphine tried to crawl away, but the beast had a firm grip on her leg. Delphine twisted and flung out her sword at the creature, stabbing it in the chest.

The lion let go of Delphine's leg and retreated back a few steps, with blood now pouring down the front of its body. Delphine reached down for the stone once again, and threw it over her head, striking the animal in the side. Her aim was dead on, likely from weeks of practicing a similar exercise in training.

The creature was off balance and Delphine charged forward, and stabbed it in its side, causing it to fall to the ground.

I held my breath this whole time, unable to look away as I wondered if it was even possible for Delphine to make it out of this alive. The animal was now on its side, heaving, the sword protruding from its belly.

As Delphine reached down to pull out the sword again, the lion swiped her paw at Delphine, catching her on her side and sending her splaying to the ground. It hissed and Delphine struggled to get up for a moment.

Micah and I were screaming, and so was everyone else around us.

Delphine scrambled up and charged at the animal again as the beast attempted to stand. She pulled the sword quickly out of the creature's flesh and then plunged it in again, and then again, each time the creature was less able to defend itself.

I saw that the lion was growing weaker, and Delphine breathed heavily, trying to catch her breath. Not wanting to take any chances, she took the sword and stabbed at the back of the lion's neck, the final blow causing it to growl one more time before becoming still.

Delphine then collapsed next to the animal, and laid her body across it, like she was protecting it from the perverse cheers of the crowd.

She looked up at Gareth angrily, who was clapping, obviously in awe of Delphine's ability to escape the situation alive and relatively unscathed.

A team of White Suits came through the gate and took away the deceased Suit on a gurney. They then lifted Delphine off of the lion's body and loaded the dead creature back into the cage, and wheeled it away, leaving Delphine alone in the middle of the Coliseum floor.

"Wonderful job, my dear Delphine!" Gareth called out. Even Chelsea was cheering in appreciation of the fight that Delphine had just won.

"Come on up here, love. I want you to be by my side for the rest of today's battles. But first, we'll have a doctor clean you up," Gareth instructed and I saw Delphine shake her head no. As White Suits grabbed onto her, she struggled to pull away, but her leg was too injured and she couldn't put weight on it. I knew if Gareth wanted her by his side, that's where she'd be.

As she was being carried out on a gurney, she looked up at Micah and me and yelled out "Help me! Please!"

There was no way to do anything for her now. I'd have to beat Odin, and then figure out how we were going to contact my dad. Then I'd get Delphine. There were many steps to figure out before I could do anything at all.

CHAPTER 13

I imagined I was next to fight, even though Ames hadn't summoned me yet. I looked over at Odin, who was calm and relaxed. He was laughing with the kid next to him, Igor, and didn't appear rattled in the least that he was going to be up for battle today, and that he was facing me.

He caught my glance and smiled and nodded his head in acknowledgment. There was no denying for either of us that we'd be facing each other soon enough, and he didn't look intimidated at all.

"Dude . . . you got this," Micah whispered under his breath.

Just then, Ames approached and pointed at me.

"Reed, you're coming with me now," he said, and a Suit grabbed my arm to start pulling me down the stairs.

"That's not necessary, I'm coming," I said, and shot Odin one more glare as I followed Ames down the stairs. Max stood by Odin now, ready to accompany him down to the prep rooms as well.

The Suit brought me into the prep room, which was dark and lined with candles that hung from the walls. Ames looked over at the Suit with an annoyed expression.

"We're good now. Please just wait right outside. I need to speak to Reed privately about what he's about to face," he said and the Suit raised his eyebrows, but let go of my arm and shuffled outside the room, closing the heavy door behind him.

Once we were alone, Ames walked over to the large metal chest on the opposite side of the room, opened the heavy door, and pulled out a long, shiny sword. It glinted yellow in the candlelight,

and when Ames brought it over to me, I saw that the entire handle was lined in sparkling emeralds.

He handed the sword to me and it was much heavier than I expected. I tried to look confident and assured with it in my hand, but I felt like a kid holding something meant for grownups.

"Are you ready for today?" Ames asked, grabbing my shoulder and looking me straight in the eye.

"Yeah, as ready as I could possibly be, I suppose. Ames, can I ask you something?"

He shook his head yes.

"Why do you want to leave the island? Aren't you treated very well here?" I asked.

He thought for a moment and then responded.

"It's true. I'm treated well. Especially because Gareth trusts me. I get everything I could possibly need here—wealth, power, etcetera, but the one thing I really want most of all, I can't have," he said.

"What's that?"

"My family," he responded.

"But why did you leave them?"

"I owed debts, and was tricked into coming here. And once I was here, I realized that Gareth would never let me leave alive, which angered me a great deal. No amount of money or luxury will replace my wife and my child," he said.

I was quiet, as I definitely didn't leave my parents on good terms. And now, there was a possibility I'd never see them again and that they may never know my true fate. I felt really shitty for that.

"I'm going to help you get to see your family again. I know you and Elise are working on a plan, but Chelsea said she had a way to contact my dad, to help us escape," I blurted out and he looked at me, surprised.

"Are you sure?" he asked.

"Yes, that is what she told me. I need to win this, so we can all get out of here."

Ames looked disturbed. "Did you say something to her about our plans?"

"No. Of course not," I lied. "She told me she wants to escape."

"That is impossible, Reed. Chelsea is on Gareth's side. She's lying to you."

I didn't believe it. "No, she knows how to help us. We have a plan," I said.

"What is it?" Ames asked.

"Chelsea's going to help me beat Odin."

Just then, Ames's wristlet lit up again and a bell outside rang loudly. The door swung open and the Suit who brought me down was waiting there with an unamused look on his face.

"Time to go," he said.

"But first, listen to my advice, Reed," Ames said sternly and looked at the Suit. He couldn't say more with the guy standing right there. He nodded at the guy, who walked out the room, ahead of us.

"Odin's weakness is that he's a show off," Ames said as we went back up the stairs. "That's the best I can give you. You're going to have to figure out the rest on your own, I'm afraid."

We got to the metal gate. I heard the crowd's heaving cheers behind the door and tried to calm myself.

Was this it? My arm shook holding the heavy sword and I felt sick to my stomach.

CHAPTER 14

I wasn't sure if Chelsea's plan was going to work. It was counting on Odin being distracted enough for me to make my move and kill him. But, after seeing Odin fight and how talented he was, I had no other options. I didn't think I could take him out without some sort of trickery. Suddenly, I didn't feel great about it, but this plan would have to do.

Ames held onto my shoulder as the gate rose slowly. Even though a White Suit was behind me to push me forward, I walked into the ring voluntarily, my head held high, resolute to look strong and without fear.

"REED! REED! REED!" The crowd

cheered, and I scanned the floor. Odin was not out yet. I walked to the center, underneath where Gareth and Chelsea were sitting.

I looked up at them and Chelsea wouldn't make eye contact with me. She was biting her nails and looked miserable and nervous. Gareth leaned into her and whispered something in her ear and she finally glanced down and nodded her head in my direction, smiling slightly and then I saw her raise her right hand and rest it against her heart, tapping it lightly.

It was a sign. I just knew it. She couldn't call down to me, or blow me a kiss, or proclaim her love to me. Her dad forbade it, the crowd wouldn't approve it, and she had to be very careful not to give any indication that we were in on a plan together. But when she tapped her heart in my direction, I felt ever so slightly better about everything. Aside from Gareth, she understood the island and Odin better than anyone, and she

knew how we'd get out of this situation alive. I had to trust her.

Just then, the gate opened yet again, and Odin strode in. I turned to face him, not wanting to look scared.

In his hand, he carried a gold-plated sword that had become his go-to weapon. He had used it during several fights, and he swung it around confidently as he approached me.

We weren't allowed to attack each other until Gareth gave us the go ahead. There was a man perched with a bow and arrow just twenty yards away who could take either of us out with one quick shot if we tried to make a move before Gareth's orders.

Odin eyed me and I stared back at him. Half the crowd chanted my name and the other half chanted Odin's, like it was some sort of game show.

I saw Odin look up toward Gareth and Chelsea and he gave a half-smile, his unapologetic cockiness on full display. Some of the people in the crowd loved him and others booed loudly. The electricity in the crowd was undeniable. Everyone was excited for an epic battle—Odin's last and he could supposedly be free.

Gareth finally spoke, and the crowd went quiet.

"This is the match-up I think we've all been waiting for. A rising star versus our most brutal and successful veteran. One fighting for his freedom and the other fighting for his life. Two of our most gifted athletes, and they have quite the friendly rivalry in training, don't we, boys?" Gareth looked down at both of us and smiled.

Odin shrugged and I nodded, "Yes sir."

"Today is going to work a little bit differently," he said, and then paused. We both waited, and the crowd grew quiet, anxious to hear what sort of trick he may have up his sleeve. Each of you is going to start at opposite sides of the Ring. When I say go, you'll each race to kill the Suit over there," he said, and pointed to the one with the bow and arrow. "That is Lex," he said, and on cue, on screen, there was a close-up of the gigantic, overly muscular Suit holding up his bow. His face was expressionless, but I could see his arm was shaking. Gareth continued talking. "Lex disobeyed me and tried to contact the outside world, so now he's part of the game today," he said. "And to make sure he stays in line, we have that Suit over there ready to go," he said, pointing across the way to another man who was aiming an arrow at Lex.

"After I say 'go,' Lex will only have permission to use his hands to defend himself. But, if he can survive for only one minute, I'll let him live and I'll also dock one win off the tally of Reed and Odin's wins. So Odin might not be leaving so quickly after all," he said.

"What do you mean?" Odin yelled out. "That's not right! I earned my nine wins fair and square," he cried and people started booing him.

Gareth shushed everyone so he could continue talking. "But, if you kill Lex within the minute, then you keep your win count intact and your battle begins immediately. Make sense?" Gareth asked.

Everyone clapped.

"One last thing," Gareth said, peering down at us. "No swords today, just hands. Put them down or my man over there will shoot. You too Lex— time to drop your weapon."

He waited as we reluctantly put our swords on the ground.

"So, are we ready to begin? Boys—get to your starting points," and two Suits escorted both of us to opposite sides of the stadium floor. Lex moved toward the middle, pivoting back and forth with arms raised. He was huge and muscular, like a professional wrestler, and I was pretty certain I couldn't take him out on my own. Odin and I would need to work together—and then for what? Just to fight each other anyway, and for me to trick him in hopes to buy more time and get out of here with Chelsea. So many things had to go right.

I considered my options, looking at Lex and then at Odin. Odin sneered at me. I glanced up at Chelsea, but she was staring off into the distance, like she was concentrating on something.

With this new twist, was our plan still in place? When would Chelsea jump down? And how would this mess up our strategy? I was just beneath where she sat, and she wouldn't meet my eyes. I'd have to trust her that she'd know what to do.

As the men in the crowd grew more frenzied, Gareth spoke again. "Okay, boys, the time is now. The clock is set and ready to go," he said, pointing to the jumbo screen. "As of now, there's nothing left to say. Go for it," and a loud firework went off, spurring us into action.

I ran forward, sprinting as fast as I could toward Lex. I saw Odin sprinting as well, and we both got within feet of Lex at the same time, who swung his arms out as I reached him. His fist made contact with my jaw and I stumbled backwards, falling to the ground. As I stood up, I saw Odin was on top of Lex's back, and he was squeezing his neck hard, anger in his eyes. As I ran forward, Odin yelled at me, even as he was squeezing the life out of Lex. It looked surprisingly easy for him.

"Get back, Reed! This one's mine!" he screamed. I didn't relish the idea of getting any closer, and thought I should conserve my energy anyway for whatever was to come next. As Lex struggled to escape, Odin clenched harder and harder until Lex finally collapsed to the ground. That was the end of it.

I stood there, backing up slowly, and tried to prepare for Odin, who released Lex's body and got up.

Chelsea's and my plan had to work; I didn't have a chance against Odin without any weapons.

Without another moment to consider every-thing, I saw Odin charging at me without hesitation, fury wrenching his face as he strode up and grabbed me, throwing me against the wall directly under where Chelsea and Gareth sat.

We were pressed up against the wall and Odin had his forearm dug into my throat, cutting off my breath. Suddenly, I saw Chelsea tumble down, and she grabbed onto Odin's back, trying to pull him off of me.

Distracted, he looked up at her, and I grabbed her, according to plan and pulled her a step away. I dragged her to where I had dropped my sword, and I reached down and grabbed it, and put the blade to her neck.

I heard the crowd screaming and Gareth yelling down at me frantically.

White Suits were now encircling us, coming down from their positions flanking the aisles of the stands, but I pressed the blade against Chelsea, my back against the wall.

Odin looked at me and smiled for a split second.

CHAPTER 15

"Go ahead. Do it!" Odin said, taunting me.

I looked at him surprised, and wasn't sure what to do.

This wasn't going according to plan. He was supposed to be caught off guard and coming to Chelsea's rescue. I held the sword against Chelsea, trying to decide if he was just playing a deadly game of chicken.

"Help me!" Chelsea screamed and Odin stood there, unmoving. "He's going to kill me!"

I looked around at everyone as they started to move in closer. I released Chelsea and held up my hands, dropping my weapon.

"I'm not going to hurt her!" I yelled out and Gareth called everyone back.

"Chelsea, get up here right now!" he screamed out, as if seeing through his daughter's trick. "Everyone's here for a good fight, and that's what we're going to see."

As Chelsea was lifted back into her seating area by two Suits that reached down to grab her outstretched arms, Odin charged forward at me. I tried to dodge out of the way, but he threw me to the ground. He got on top of me easily and I found myself unable to move under his weight.

He put his hands around my neck and began to squeeze the life out of me. *Okay, this is it. This is going to be how I go*, I thought.

But just as I was beginning to pass out, Gareth yelled down. "Really, Odin? You think I'll let you out of here that easy? It's making me think I may need you to fight again, so everyone gets their money's worth."

Odin hesitated and looked down at me,

annoyed. I could tell he was considering his options.

The crowd booed and taunted him, throwing down food and rocks at us.

"Fine!" Odin yelled, and got up off of me and turned and walked toward his sword, which was lying in the dirt on the other side of the stadium.

As he pivoted, I stumbled upright and lunged at my own sword, lying in the dirt just feet away. The crowd screamed. Weak on my feet, I hobbled toward Odin, gaining my footing as I reached him. I swung my sword outward at him, stabbing him in the back.

He screamed out in pain and spun back to me, looking surprised for just a split second before reaching down to snatch up his own sword. He faced me and threw the sword hard in my direc-tion, like a dart. I moved to the left and it nicked my right arm, catching at my elbow and causing blood to spurt out. I dropped my sword and yelled out in pain before ducking down to grab Odin's weapon with the other arm.

I looked up and Odin was now holding a scythe in his hand, its curved metal tip gleaming in the sun. I saw the dead White Suit right behind him and realized he'd stolen the weapon away. I glanced up at Gareth, who was smiling and didn't seem interested in stopping what was happening.

Odin raised the scythe and started charging toward me. His weapon was much longer than mine. I tried to think quickly as he raised the scythe to strike me. It came down and I moved the sword in my right hand upward, cutting the top of the scythe off in one fell motion, the sharp tip scattering across the dirt floor.

The crowd screamed—I could hear Chelsea the loudest—and as Odin scrambled to recover, I moved forward quickly and hit him across the left arm with my blade, taking it clean off at the elbow. He screamed and looked back at me, shocked.

He stumbled to the ground, grabbing at his

stumpy arm with his good one, and I moved forward, lunging toward him quickly. Before Odin had time to recover, I swung the sword down, splitting his head open. He collapsed before me and I heard a loud, painful wail behind me. It was Chelsea.

CHAPTER 16

Odin died instantly, and the crowd erupted into wild cheers. I dropped the sword, shocked that I was able to kill Odin, and all because he didn't take me out when he had a clear shot. He was always such a show-off, and that was his real vulnerability, just like Ames said. I should be dead right now, not him.

Gareth suddenly started speaking and I looked up at him. Chelsea wasn't beside him any longer. Where was she? Where did she go?

Gareth didn't seem to notice—or care—and was applauding wildly.

"Bravo, Reed. Bravo! That was quite dramatic, wasn't it? I was nervous there for a second that we'd have our first ten-win fighter, and I'd have to set him free."

The camera zoomed in to Gareth's face and he gave an almost imperceptible wink, like he had something caught in his eye, causing the crowd to laugh. "But Reed stepped up in the face of adversity and rose to the challenge."

As he talked, the screen showed my face in extreme close up and I looked like a different person, hollow and mean, glaring at the camera.

"Today, Reed is well on his way to freedom. It will be interesting to see what he does when he gets close to leaving. Hopefully he'll be a little bit wiser than poor Odin, isn't that right Chelsea?"

Gareth turned to his right and Chelsea wasn't there. He looked perplexed for a moment, and then annoyed.

"Oh, don't mind her. She's just a typical teenager. Boo hoo hoo . . . " Gareth said, before continuing, "Now Reed, I'm going to allow you a special treat today as a reward for your performance. Pick any of my girls or boys—whatever suits you, to spend the evening with—" he pointed to an area where several pretty girls and half-dressed men were sitting, looking down at me smiling.

"No, that's okay. I'll pass," I said, disgusted. I needed to find Chelsea to figure out what had happened.

Gareth looked annoyed, but said. "Well, suit yourself. More fun for everyone else then."

I was starting to feel a little woozy, too. I glanced down and saw a large pool of blood gathering around me, dripping down my hand off of my injured arm.

I sat down on the dirt, and waited for the stretcher, which came out just moments later.

I got onto it voluntarily and was taken back through the hallway to the medical treatment room. On the way, we passed Ames in the hallway. He looked down at me with an "I told you so" look, but he said, "Good job, brother. You did well out there. I'll see you on the other side soon."

I couldn't talk to him because I was taken down the hallway before I was able to respond.

I was brought into the medical room where Darby was waiting for me.

"Where's Elise? I want to see Elise," I said, anxious to talk to her.

"Why are you so curious about Elise?"

"I just prefer talking to girls, that's all," I said, feeling defensive.

He took a look at my wound, which was deep, the sword shaving off a chunk of my forearm and elbow. The pain was becoming worse as the adrenaline wore off and I cringed and called out in pain when he tended to the wound with some sort of mysterious white, thick paste.

He handed me some pills and a drink.

"Take these. They'll help with the pain."

"What is this?" I questioned, starting to feel worse and worse.

"Ibuprofen. Extra strength. What else?" Darby said as he was peering down at the wound with a light on his headband.

"Fuck it," I said and took the medicine, hoping to take the edge off. Almost instantaneously, I felt a little bit better. Then, I started to get woozy again until I couldn't sit upright and the room felt like it was spinning, so I lay back on the table.

"What is this? It's not ibuprofen . . . " I mumbled.

"It'll help you sleep, Reed."

I felt my eyes growing heavy and I soon felt very tired. I was asleep, but started to stir awake when a repetitive noise echoed in my ear. I heard someone talking to me and I became confused. Where was I? My head felt strange and I wondered if I was still drugged.

"Wake up, Reed. Wake up," I opened my eyes and Chelsea was sitting next to my bed. I didn't feel pain any longer as she leaned into me, and her face looked even more beautiful than I'd ever seen it before. Her long hair glowed with the light of the room above her head, and I swear she was the closest thing to an angel I'd ever seen.

I was woozy and wondered if I was seeing double.

"You came for me," I said, my voice weak. "What happened out there?"

"I'm so sorry, Reed. I never imagined Odin would react the way he did."

I looked at her, not sure if I could trust her.

"Do you forgive me? Please?" She looked at me with her big doe eyes and I tried to concentrate on her face.

"I don't know . . ."

"Please. We can get out of here together. Let's run away," I felt her seductive persuasiveness starting to work on me.

"I'm not . . ."

She got on top of me, straddling me, and I was too weak to push her off.

"You want this, don't you?"

She looked at me with pleading eyes and I couldn't disagree. Of course I wanted it. I wanted her the moment I laid eyes on her.

"Yes . . . yes . . . " I sounded off and she moved on top of me. My whole world felt different than before. The colors of the room changed, the walls fell away, and it felt like we were floating.

"Let's get out of here, baby," she said as she leaned down, her hair falling on my bare chest. I didn't feel any sadness at all; I was the happiest I'd ever been.

All the pain of the last two years fell away and I was just in this moment and there was no island. There was no Oregon. There was no home except here with Chelsea on top of me.

"I think I love you . . . " I felt myself say and didn't feel embarrassed or ashamed. I looked up at her, eager to hear her say it back. But when I reached up to touch her hips, she wasn't there.

The room was very dark and I sat up, confused. Where was I? Where had Chelsea gone?

I realized I was on the medical table, where Darby had tended to me, and I had passed out. My head was very heavy and throbbing, and I felt dizzy.

That had all just been a dream, I realized. I was furious. The hallucination was the happiest and most at peace I'd felt for such a long time—and it wasn't real at all. It was the product of some drug cocktail probably prescribed to subdue me.

I tried to think through everything that happened in the Coliseum, as it had gone so horribly wrong. Where was Chelsea now?

I suddenly remembered her scream as I took out Odin—a pained howl that rose up above the crowd's cheers and pierced me at the core.

It became obvious all of a sudden. Odin was the one that Chelsea loved. It seemed so clear now. I thought they were ex-lovers, but she screamed for him, not me. She was trying to protect him.

But why the hell did she toy with me? And why didn't Odin kill me? Why did she pretend to like me at all? And kiss me, and sneak out with me in the middle of the night?

I had no idea, except that she was somehow trying to be cruel to me. And to Odin. What did I do, though?

And I then thought about Elise's warning. She had told me to stay away from Chelsea, that she was trouble, and I didn't believe her. She knew a truth in her that I was blind to—her beauty had given me hope, something to be excited about and to live for here.

My foolishness made me glum and I cried out for help again and again, waiting for someone to come and check on me.

I'd attack them so I could make a break for it. What did I have to lose? No one was escaping this island alive. Ten wins was bullshit. Gareth just liked to toy with everyone and give them false hope.

It was decided. I'd kill the Suit that came next.

I'd take them out quickly and then I'd hide out on the island until I could find Ames or Elise.

They'd have to accelerate the plan to get out of here. And when we left, the island would be in ruins. I'd burn this whole place down on the way out, happily leaving Chelsea and Gareth behind.

I fantasized about everything burning to the ground while I waited for the door to open, knowing that my attack would catch whoever entered off guard. Now was the time to do it, before I had to fight again.

CHAPTER 17

I heard someone approach the door about an hour later. I waited on the other side and when the door swung open, I grabbed the person and covered their mouth as they shrieked.

"Reed! It's me! Elise!" she yelled out as I tried to contain her. She was writhing in my grip and I let go quickly.

"Jesus. What was that about? Do you have a death wish?" Elise hissed at me, glaring at me in the dark room.

"I'm sorry . . . I thought you were going to be a Suit or Darby."

"About that—you need to keep your mouth

shut. Darby is wondering why you keep asking about me. Are you stupid?"

"No. I'm fed up. I'm going to get killed if we don't start the escape plan soon."

"I know, Reed. We had to gather more support before we could begin. But I think we're almost ready."

"Where's Chelsea?"

It felt like a stupid question, but I couldn't help but ask.

"Reed. I told you to stay away from her." Elise looked at me disappointed. "She's devastated and out for your head."

"What do you mean?"

"Odin was Chelsea's love and you killed the only thing that she had to live for."

"Why did she hang out with me then? Why did she kiss me?"

"They were having a stupid lovers' quarrel, that's it. It only lasted a few weeks, and Chelsea was using you to make Odin jealous and mad.

And it worked, right? Odin loved making your life miserable."

"Wait—how do you know all this?"

"I've known Chelsea for many years and have a soft spot for the poor girl. When I realized she and Odin liked each other years ago, I helped them have a relationship behind Gareth's back. And then I continued protecting them and their relationship as long as I could. Then you came into the picture and mucked everything up," Elise looked at me, annoyed.

"But what happened in the Coliseum?" I asked. "She said she'd help me. That was a trick?"

"Yes, Reed," Elise said, exasperated. "You're just putting this together? Odin was threatened by you. Not only because of Chelsea, but because you were the new Praeclarus darling . . . and Gareth loves watching you, too. Chelsea made sure Odin knew that. But then, they got back together and as soon as they knew Odin would be fighting you, they schemed to take you out. They saw you as a threat. She tricked you."

"Why are you telling me this now? Why didn't you come help me?"

"I've been locked away, Reed. Gareth suspected I was trying to help Odin, and was punishing me. But, after Odin died, he let me out," Elise explained. "That was only a few hours ago."

She continued, "I came here as soon as I had a chance to do so undetected. And I can't stay long. If a Suit comes in, we're both dead. I was taken off tending to prisoners. It would be very fishy."

"Okay. So what's the plan? How can I help?"

"Ames and a small team have hacked into the island's computer system. He thinks he has a way to contact your dad, but he needs you to be there, to communicate with him directly. Your dad needs to know that you're alive and that it's not some scam. Then your dad is going to need to send a search party. I know the approximate location of the island, but not specifics. And Gareth has blocked satellite imagery, so the island doesn't show up on digital maps. Your dad will need to send people to help before anyone on the island suspects anything fishy is going on." Elise continued, "And, if they do, we have to be ready to fight. We've gathered many staff members that are prepared to revolt. And I assume the prisoners are on our side too. We can rally them too."

"Totally," I said, agreeing that the fighters would battle for freedom, if given the opportunity.

"But Gareth has an arsenal of weapons that we haven't even seen yet. I imagine he'll unleash all his power to stop anyone from escaping. He's vowed that he'll take out the island and everyone on it if he's faced with being caught. And I believe him. We need to be very careful about how we proceed," Elise said.

I thought about everything carefully. Was this a trap, too? But why would Elise do that? I really didn't know what to believe.

"So when does this all go down?"

"Ames thinks he can get to the computer motherboard tomorrow night, during the Praeclarus feast. But we're going to have to figure out how to break you free without causing alarm."

We heard footsteps coming down the hallway quickly. Elise swore under her breath. "Shit."

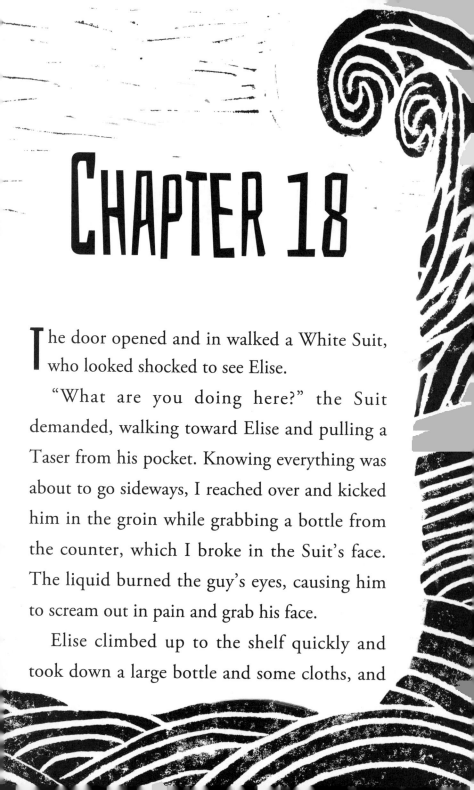

CHAPTER 18

The door opened and in walked a White Suit, who looked shocked to see Elise.

"What are you doing here?" the Suit demanded, walking toward Elise and pulling a Taser from his pocket. Knowing everything was about to go sideways, I reached over and kicked him in the groin while grabbing a bottle from the counter, which I broke in the Suit's face. The liquid burned the guy's eyes, causing him to scream out in pain and grab his face.

Elise climbed up to the shelf quickly and took down a large bottle and some cloths, and clamped it over the Suit's nose, causing him to collapse to the ground.

"We gotta hurry. He'll only be passed out for a few hours. Let's go," Elise demanded, grabbing me as we stepped over the body into the hallway. She closed the heavy door behind us, and then pulled on the handle, checking that it was locked shut. She looked to the right and left and then we darted down long hallways until we got to the same door Chelsea had led me out of weeks before.

"We have to conceal you."

It was the middle of the night, but we needed to find a place for me to hide out before morning came and the Suit woke up.

"I have to get back to my post shortly or it'll arouse suspicions," Elise said.

"Don't worry, I know where to go," I said, looking up at the path Chelsea had taken me on before. It was silent and the only light came from the sporadic lamp posts dotted along the trail that snaked up the hill.

"Where should I meet you? When? I don't have a watch," I said, trying to figure out how to evade detection for twenty-four hours.

"Do you know where the airplane hangar is?" Elise asked.

"Yes, approximately," I said.

"Good. Meet us there by the northern entrance at sundown tomorrow," Elise commanded and I nodded. "And, if you get caught, do not give Ames or me up, okay?"

She looked at me, wanting to make sure I understood.

"Of course," I responded.

"Be very careful, Reed, and don't do anything stupid," Elise said before turning and running back through the door from which we had come.

I didn't have time to think things through, but I knew I needed to get up the mountain, far from the normal patrol area of the Suits and the strolling locations of Praeclarus members. I realized that if I was going to run, this was the point of no return. If I was caught, I'd surely be killed.

I turned around and started walking quickly up the path, looking around nervously at every odd noise. I didn't encounter anyone, and thankfully there was no moon in the sky tonight so it was very dark.

I slipped between the lights illuminating the path, weaving up the hill and past the lookout point. I stopped for a moment and studied the exact location of the airplane hangar. I saw a road leading to it from the Coliseum. I needed to get to that road tomorrow, undetected. It would be very difficult, especially if Gareth and the Suits knew I was missing by that point.

I realized I couldn't stay in this spot. I was too exposed, so I kept on moving, going down the backside of the path quickly, and keeping my eye out for any surprise encounters.

Finally, I got to the game reserve, which was very dark; it wasn't lit up like everywhere else on the island. I found an area with very long grass next to the tiger area and laid down in it, trying to pull the weeds over me. The tiger heard me, though, and seemed to be distressed by the sudden movement. It snarled and I heard it come up to the fence, growling and breathing heavily as it sniffed the air.

I just needed to stay very still and undetected until midday tomorrow. I tried not to think about the animals—I was safer here at the reserve than anywhere on the main part of the island.

I sat there as still as I could for as long as I could stand it, but the grass was very cold and wet and itchy and I felt miserable. I felt sick knowing Chelsea had been playing me this whole time—I was such an idiot, falling for her plan so easily.

I suddenly heard someone approaching, taking slow steps in my direction.

Was it an animal out of its cage? Was it a Suit? Or Gareth who knew I was loose and was coming to kill me himself?

The footsteps were very, very slow and I tried not to breathe or move too much and hoped the thing, whatever it was, would walk right by me.

The steps got closer and closer and then stopped right next to me. I held my breath and prayed for the first time since arriving at the island. The tension of not knowing what was above me was too much to bear, so I opened my eyes and through the long blades of grass, I saw Chelsea standing above me, looking down.

She had an angry look on her face and she bent down and pulled me up out of the grass and onto my feet. I looked around but she seemed to be alone.

"That was way too easy, Reed. I knew I'd find you here," she said, sounding annoyed.

"How did you know I was missing?"

"I went to the medical room and found the Suit passed out on the floor. Good job, by the way—that was impressive," she said sarcastically.

"And when I figured you were missing, I

thought you might come here. You saw there were no patrols up here at night, and you knew the way. So, I put two and two together, and voila, here you are."

She glared at me and I didn't know what to say. I looked down and she was holding a long dagger in her right hand. I was weaponless and I glanced around to see if there was anything in sight that I could grab to take her out, if it came to that.

"So, are you going to kill me now?" I asked, pointing down to the weapon.

"I'm not a killer, Reed, unlike you," she said angrily. "This is for self-defense, just in case," she said, pointing the dagger at me. "Don't make me have to use it," she spat at me.

"You tricked me, Chelsea," I said.

I was falling in love with her, and that was all fake. She and Odin had conspired to kill me, but she was going to have him do the dirty work.

"You were easy to trick," Chelsea said. "But I've found men typically are. Let's move it. I'm taking you now to see Gareth, and I'll let him figure out how to punish you."

She waved her dagger at me forcefully and we started down the path again, this time in very different circumstances than before.

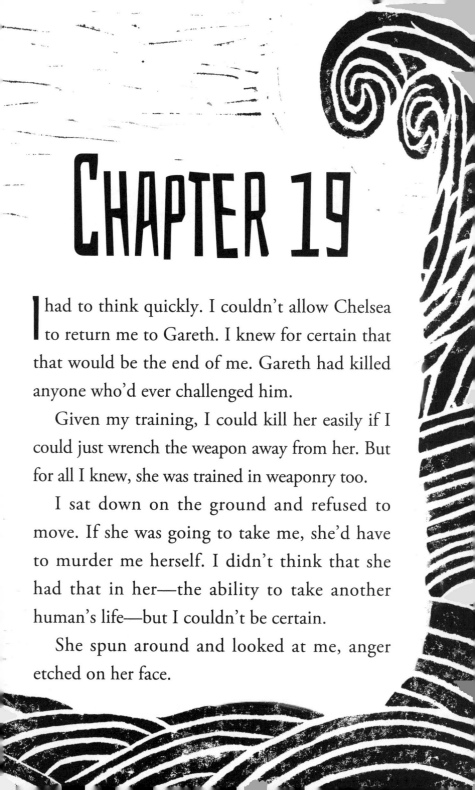

CHAPTER 19

I had to think quickly. I couldn't allow Chelsea to return me to Gareth. I knew for certain that that would be the end of me. Gareth had killed anyone who'd ever challenged him.

Given my training, I could kill her easily if I could just wrench the weapon away from her. But for all I knew, she was trained in weaponry too.

I sat down on the ground and refused to move. If she was going to take me, she'd have to murder me herself. I didn't think that she had that in her—the ability to take another human's life—but I couldn't be certain.

She spun around and looked at me, anger etched on her face.

"What are you doing? Let's go."

"No. I'm not moving."

"Yes you are. Come with me now," she ordered and started to walk back toward me, dagger raised.

"You going to kill me?" I asked, challenging her. "You're good at heart, Chelsea, I know it. Don't do it."

I saw her hesitate for just a second. "You murdered Odin!" she screamed at me, waving the weapon in front of her face. "You killed the only person I'll ever love. You took him from me!"

Tears were welling up in her eyes and I wasn't sure what she'd do. She looked furious.

"Why did you do it, Chelsea? Why did you pretend to like me?"

"I wanted to make Odin jealous. We were in a fight, but that was stupid. Then, when we made up, we agreed we had to take you out. It was getting complicated."

"What do you mean?" I asked, trying to understand what was going on.

"Odin and you couldn't co-exist on the island. There can be only be one star. It was only a matter of time until you faced each other in the Round."

"So why did you come onto the Coliseum floor?" I asked.

"To turn Gareth against you," Chelsea said, like it was plainly obvious.

"Why would you need to do that?"

"Gareth has always hated Odin. He never approved of him, especially when he figured out what was going on with us. We were convinced Gareth's plan was ultimately to spare you and kill Odin."

She continued, tears falling down her face, "Gareth was a huge fan of yours, and that ate at Odin. It made him very angry. So, we figured if we could make it seem like you were going to kill me, Gareth would turn on you right there and order your imminent death."

"But it didn't work that way, did it?" I questioned.

Chelsea looked mad.

I kept talking, wanting her to see the truth. "You can still join our side, Chelsea. I know you are different from your dad—I see the good in you. And we can get out of here . . . together . . . " I said, trying to calm her.

Chelsea was silent, thinking.

I contemplated what to do next. I didn't believe Chelsea was inherently bad, but that she was raised by a real monster, a man that taught her that trickery was commonplace.

"You can still escape, Chelsea. You can leave this all behind."

"No, Reed, it's impossible. How are you going to do that? Tell me the real plan, not just some empty promises . . . "

I wasn't sure what to say—I couldn't trust her, but I wanted her to believe that I was being sincere.

"Uhh . . . " I said, trying to figure out what to say next without giving anything more away.

Chelsea burst out laughing.

"What's so funny?" I demanded.

"No one gets out of here alive, Reed. No one. Many have tried, so whatever you're thinking, I doubt you're smarter than everyone else that's attempted to escape and been killed," Chelsea responded. "Besides, where are you going to go?" she asked, looking down at me with a smirk.

"I'll go home."

"That's hilarious, Reed. Your parents think you're dead. They've already had your funeral. You have a gravestone already, right next to your drowned brother," she said.

"What do you mean?" I asked, my stomach dropping. Was that true? And if so, why was she telling me this? Just to be cruel?

"Yeah, my dad showed me the article online. He thought it was funny," she said nonchalantly. "Your boat went down in the ocean. They found the wreckage, but no survivors."

"Why are you saying this to me?" I asked her and she just smiled.

"You caused me the greatest pain I could ever imagine, taking Odin away from me. Now I am going to do the same."

"So, you are just like your dad?"

"I'm not like him at all, but I'm going to avenge Odin's death," she said.

"Then you're going to have to stop me," I spat at her and got up, running as quickly I could away, toward the fence around the game area. I heard Chelsea swear as she started running after me.

"Stop, Reed!" she yelled. It was still dark, but dawn was beginning and the sky was a muddy brownish-black. I could barely see in front of me and I charged through the tall grass, running as fast I could. I got to the fence and turned the corner, and glanced back. Chelsea was about twenty yards away. As I looked at her, she stumbled and screamed out as she fell on her face.

"Fucking asshole. I'm going to get you, Reed," she yelled as she stood up.

I kept on running and turned to the left, going into the trees that lined the edge of the game area.

I heard Chelsea screaming, but her voice was getting further and further away.

"I'm going to make sure you pay for killing Odin! If he couldn't get off the island alive, neither will you!"

That was the last I heard from her. I kept on sprinting through the thick trees and down a hill. This felt like the uninhabited part of the island, as I didn't see any signs of development at all—no trails, no lamp posts, no buildings, nothing.

Where would this lead? It was far from the meet-up point Ames and Elise had given me, but I knew I couldn't turn back.

The trees started to thin out a little bit, and through the clearing, I saw the ocean. I ran until I got to the shoreline and stopped. There was nowhere left for me to go.

I looked out at the ocean and wondered where in the world we were. Was Chelsea telling the truth about my parents? Were they not even looking for me?

I thought about my mom believing I was dead and how shitty it was that she'd never know anything different if I couldn't escape. I was lost to the water, just like James.

There was no other land in sight. I tried to calculate how long it would take my dad to get ships or airplanes to us to help. Would there be enough time between when we alerted him to evade being killed by Gareth?

I knew Chelsea was probably running back to Gareth now.

I wondered how I'd get to the hangar without being detected. Every Suit would be out searching for me come sunrise.